Selected Praise for Priscila Uppal's Works

Projection: Encounters with My Runaway Mother

"*Projection* proves to be remarkably free of self-pity ... [A] raw, passionate memoir, a fierce exercise in family exorcism."
— *Montreal Gazette*

"Uppal is brave ... made of sterner stuff than most; an inspiration to messed-up adult children everywhere."
— *Globe and Mail*

"[S]uperbly conveyed without any excessive literary artifice ... *Projection* is a book that's simultaneously cerebral and visceral, and its ardent refusal of any sort of mind-body split — to sacrifice sophistication for sentiment or vice versa — is the sign of an author who has thrown herself wholly into her book."
— *National Post*

"Incorporating movie and pop-culture references as storytelling devices is what makes this book truly shine ... Above all, Uppal is an impeccable writer, deftly infusing complex scenes and emotions with power and weight ... a worthy read."
— *Quill & Quire*

"[A] heartbreaking memoir."
—*Toronto Life*

"Intimate, sad, probing and self-aware, often very funny logbook of a harrowing encounter."
— *Literary Review of Canada*

To Whom It May Concern

"It is to be hoped that Uppal will continue to rival Atwood in productivity and wit. As Shakespeare might have said: Fortune, smile again on lovers of CanLit; grace us with more irresistible stories from Uppal's unique perspective."

— *Montreal Gazette*

"Uppal is a deep thinker, capable of carefully peeling back layer upon layer of the human psyche ... makes us laugh and cry long after the last page of the novel has been read."

— *Ottawa Citizen*

"Uppal's writing bursts with humour, plot turns and insights ... Uppal should be congratulated for writing one of the most powerful and riskiest scenes in a Canadian novel ... [she] reveals herself as a compassionate and perspicacious novelist whose humanity and intelligence cannot be overlooked."

— *Globe and Mail*

The Divine Economy of Salvation

"In its confident voice and its unsparing, concisely powerful narrative — like Margaret Laurence at her best — *Divine Economy* is an impressive debut."

— *Globe and Mail*

"A luminous debut ... haunting, gripping, and surprisingly nuanced: begins as a simple mystery and turns into a work of great depth and seriousness."

— *Kirkus* starred review

Cover Before Striking

Striking

stories

PRISCILA UPPAL

DUNDURN

TORONTO

Editor: Shannon Whibbs
Interior Design: Colleen Wormald
Cover Design: Laura Boyle
Cover Image: matchbox © iStockPhoto/ Krasyuk
Printer: Webcom

Library and Archives Canada Cataloguing in Publication

Uppal, Priscila
        Cover before striking / Priscila Uppal.

Short stories.
Title story previously published: Toronto : Lyricalmyrical
    Press, 2004.
Issued in print and electronic formats.
ISBN 978-1-4597-2952-0 (pbk.).--ISBN 978-1-4597-2953-7
(pdf).--ISBN 978-1-4597-2954-4 (epub)

        I. Title.

PS8591.P62C693 2015   C813'.54   C2014-904274-4   C2014-904275-2

1   2   3   4   5   19   18   17   16   15

Conseil des Arts
du Canada   Canada Council
for the Arts   Canadä   ONTARIO ARTS COUNCIL
CONSEIL DES ARTS DE L'ONTARIO
an Ontario government agency
un organisme du gouvernement de l'Ontario

We acknowledge the support of the **Canada Council for the Arts** and the **Ontario Arts Council** for our publishing program. We also acknowledge the financial support of the **Government of Canada** through the **Canada Book Fund** and **Livres Canada Books**, and the **Government of Ontario** through the **Ontario Book Publishing Tax Credit** and the **Ontario Media Development Corporation.**

Care has been taken to trace the ownership of copyright material used in this book. The author and the publisher welcome any information enabling them to rectify any references or credits in subsequent editions.
J. Kirk Howard, President

The publisher is not responsible for websites or their content unless they are owned by the publisher.

Printed and bound in Canada.

VISIT US AT
Dundurn.com I *@dundurnpress* I *Facebook.com/dundurnpress* I *Pinterest.com/dundurnpress*

Dundurn
3 Church Street, Suite 500
Toronto, Ontario, Canada
M5E 1M2

For Richard Teleky,
who has been here since the beginning

Also by Priscila Uppal

Memoir
Projection: Encounters with My Runaway Mother

Novels
To Whom It May Concern: A Novel
The Divine Economy of Salvation

Poetry
Sabotage
Summer Sport: Poems
Winter Sport: Poems
Successful Tragedies: Selected Poems 1998–2010
Traumatology
Ontological Necessities
Live Coverage
Pretending to Die
Confessions of a Fertility Expert
How to Draw Blood From a Stone

Criticism
*We Are What We Mourn: The Contemporary English-Canadian
Elegy*

As Editor
Best Canadian Poetry 2011
The Exile Book of Canadian Sports Stories
*The Exile Book of Poetry in Translation: Twenty Canadian Poets
Take on the World*
Barry Callaghan: Essays on His Works
Red Silk: An Anthology of South-Asian Canadian Women Poets
Uncommon Ground: A Celebration of Matt Cohen

Who, marked for failure, dulled by grief,
Has traded in his wife and friend
For this warm ledge, this alder leaf:
Comfort that does not comprehend.

— Edna St. Vincent Millay, "The Return"

Contents

Recipes for Dirty Laundry

Animal Stains: Apply vinegar and baking soda; then scrub.

Rosa knows Teresa is the pretty one: she has more problems. Today it's the bath. Water running, Rosa knows Teresa will be pouring in some of the red bubble bath that smells like raspberries her sister always finds enough money for when it's on sale. Sometimes Rosa uses it, too, waiting patiently until all the bubbles disappear before calling for someone to take her out. Then, after Mamma or Teresa help her into a nightdress, she keeps the towel beside her, inhaling the faint scent of the berries on the cloth. Rosa only bathes on Sundays, but Teresa bathes whenever she wants.

Today the bath is a problem, Rosa can tell. Her bedroom is beside the bathroom since it's easier for her to go in the middle of the night. She can hold on to the walls until she reaches the Virgin Mary in a light blue-and-white frock, eyes and hands pointing to the heavens in prayer. It is a good picture, and Rosa, in the dark of the night, always knows which door is the right one. Today, lying down on her single bed, she can hear a faint sobbing from the Virgin Mary's direction like the hum from her old radio. She decides to get up, pushing against the guardrail for leverage.

Rosa slides her leg over the end of the bed where the guardrail doesn't intrude and puts on her brace, attaching the straps across her calves, slipping her fingers through the steel wires. She can tell where the straps should be from the marks over and under her knees, slightly darker than the rest of her skin, pressed like pleats in linen. She tries to be quiet. She doesn't want Mamma to catch her taking a peek at her sister, which she likes to do when Teresa bathes. If the door is locked, she returns to her own bed, wraps her wool blanket around her shoulders, and looks through one of her picture books, her favourite about a small girl in a red dress who meets a wolf in the forest. Resting the book across her chest, she imagines herself skipping off down a path in a forest to the washroom where Teresa is and pushing her fingers in front of her nose, imagines the smell of bubble bath or leg cream, all flowery and sweet. Then sometimes Rosa pretends to shave her legs, the way she has seen Teresa do it, propping her ankle on the bed board instead of the edge of the tub and scraping against her skin with a hairbrush. She even moans quietly, the way Teresa does once in a while, splashing the water just over her skin, hands hidden and eyes closed, cheeks flushed and breathing heavily, a sound like the soft and quick bursts made when trying to open a stuck can lid.

Rosa has to use both hands to keep her leg straight when she drops it lightly on the carpet to make her way to the washroom. She can already imagine the back of Teresa's head, her long hair like roots descending into the water, and her long naked body half-covered in bubbles. If Mamma were to come down the hallway, collecting laundry from the hampers placed just outside of each door, it would be easy to pretend she's just checking to see if she can use the bathroom. She could even hold on to the elastic waistband of her pants and wriggle her upper body a little.

Today the door is locked. Rosa frowns, but then remembers. She has an excuse to go in. Teresa is crying: she has a problem. Rosa might be able to help. She knocks. No sound, not even sobbing. Resting her head against the door, Rosa's cheeks flatten into the Virgin Mary's tight hands.

"Get away from the door, Rosa."

Rosa doesn't budge. "You're crying. I can help."

"Rosa, listen to me. I'm fine. Just get away from the door." Teresa's voice is firm, but low.

"You feel sad, Tera?" Rosa wishes she could get on the floor and peek through the crack, but she wouldn't be able to get up without help.

"Go away, Rosa. Right now!" Rosa recognizes the "I don't have time for you" voice. Teresa doesn't use it often, but when she does, Rosa is expected to obey. As she bows her head beneath the Virgin Mary's chin, her eyes begin to tear.

"Sorry, Tera. I don't mean it."

Rosa hears sniffling. "Just go and read and maybe I'll tuck you in later." Then guitars and drums, insistent and hard, blare through the door. Rosa's voice can't compete, so she ambles back to her room.

After taking off her brace and placing it neatly upright, Rosa crawls back into bed. She likes to lie down all alone, pretend she's wearing white shoes and a red dress with fancy beads, and that there's a bouquet of pink flowers by the nightstand given to her by some boy. Tonight she pretends this boy has a ticket to the school dance. Last month Teresa took her. Rosa liked handing over the ticket. "I'm here," it said to her. "Look at me." Some boys were turned away, ones with tickets, too, who smelled and walked funny. But they never turned Rosa away. Miss Brown told her she looked pretty, and Teresa bought her an orange drink at the booth, leaving Rosa with her. Rosa didn't need to go with a boy, that's just what a lot of girls did. Teresa danced with boys, close if the songs were slow, like the songs she usually liked to listen to in the bath. Before, dances had been a problem, when Teresa and Rosa were at separate schools. But now Rosa also attends the high school, though she stays in the same class, not like Teresa who spends her day moving from one room to another with different textbooks. Teresa doesn't have class with Miss Brown, but Rosa does. Miss Brown helps Rosa with her sewing, since she is one of the few allowed to sew.

"That girl's gonna get in trouble, Mamma. I had a dream—"

Papa's voice is harsh and he coughs when he yells too loud. *Mamma must be rubbing his back*, Rosa thinks. Maybe she could check, make sure Papa hasn't hurt his chest, but Mamma doesn't like it when she knocks on Papa's door without asking. "You need to be sure of his mood," Mamma told her. "He's sick."

"I'm sick, too," Rosa replied.

"No, you're not, Rosa. Don't say that again. And don't say that to the neighbours. They don't understand."

Rosa can hear Mamma stamping down the hallway. She is crying, too, and Rosa imagines a white handkerchief dangling from her fingers, grey hair hanging out the back of her net.

"Teresa. Get out of there right now!" Mamma knocks vigorously. Rosa lifts her back off the bed to get a look into the hallway. This is certainly "a commotion," what Mamma said Rosa shouldn't do outside in front of anyone, that if someone speaks to her she should pretend she can't speak English and point to the house. Maybe Mamma can't help making "a commotion"; Rosa sometimes couldn't help it. Maybe Mamma thinks the bathroom is dirty or the music is too loud.

"Just a minute, Mamma."

"Right now!"

The music stops. Hands clenched into fists, Mamma turns and thumps down the stairs. Rosa can hear the plug being pulled, the water swirling and burping down the drain, and Teresa getting out of the tub. Soon after, lock unfastened, Teresa emerges in a white terry-cloth robe, black hair frizzed up even though it is wet and should be straight and heavy. *Teresa didn't comb it*, Rosa thinks. But she always gave her hair a good combing in the bath or else it hurt the next day and Mamma would need to help her, the way Mamma always combs Rosa's hair.

"Teresa Maria Campanous!"

"One minute, Mamma! I have to get some clothes on!"

"Ha! Clothes! You better put some clothes on and keep them on —"

"Mamma, I'm coming! Please!"

"If I could walk ..." The coughing stops Papa's sentence.

Teresa halts at Rosa's door, her face red and prunish. "You go to sleep, Rosa."

Rosa nods and pulls the covers over her head, imagining herself in a car with guitar and drum music playing, wind from an open window sweeping up her hair. After fifteen minutes, Rosa wants to close her door, but doesn't want to get up. She hates it when people talk loud, but not loud enough to pass through doors. Then it's just noise and it hurts to concentrate.

A half hour later, her sister walks by again. "Tera," she whispers, but Teresa turns off the light in the bathroom and shuffles to her room at the other end of the hall.

Once again, Rosa puts on her brace and steps quietly out her door. She holds on to the walls, past the bathroom, past Papa's room, to Teresa's room. Without knocking, she inches the door open with her foot and Teresa, crouched on the floor, shoves some clothes under the bed. Looking up, Teresa sighs, but with a finger against her lips waves to Rosa to come in and quietly shut the door.

"You need those washed, Tera?"

Teresa wipes her eyes and kicks a pant leg farther underneath the bed. "No."

"I can wash them."

"No, Rosa. And don't tell Mamma." Teresa has slipped back into her bathrobe. Rosa notices how red her legs are and that the yellow sponge from the bathroom in her hand has red blotches on it.

"You cut yourself shaving? You gonna take another bath?"

Teresa doesn't answer. She gets up, sits on the edge of her bed, and pats the place beside her. Rosa sits down. Rosa likes Teresa's comforter. It's pink, like the walls.

"Pretty clothes, Tera. Can I have them, if you're gonna throw them away?" Rosa likes to get clothes from Teresa. Teresa has store-bought clothes instead of wearing only the dresses Mamma makes.

"No. They're no good. They're garbage."

Rosa gasps, knowing Mamma does not like it when they throw things in the trash.

"Good for rags then, Tera. Good for —"

"Listen, Rosa. This is important," Teresa stresses, gripping Rosa's arm. "And you don't tell Mamma."

"Okay."

Rosa concentrates, staring at the pink comforter. There are things Rosa must not tell Mamma. That's what sisters do, she knows, keep secrets. Rosa waits, but Teresa's hand starts shaking, and the sash on the white robe grows a spot of pink.

"Oh, Christ." Teresa pulls off the white robe in front of Rosa, her slim naked body with small, tight breasts and just a triangle of hair between the legs open to Rosa's eyes, presses the sponge against her thighs, then grabs a large T-shirt from the back of the closet.

"Don't say that. You're not allowed to say that. Did Mamma do that to you?"

"No." Pulling the T-shirt over her head, the hem under her thighs, she sits back on the bed, takes her pillow and lays it over her lap. "An animal did," she adds, as if to her legs and not to Rosa. Now Rosa starts to shake, imagining the wolf from her picture book, his fangs bared and growling.

"Rosa, some boys are bad. This is our secret."

"Not the boys you dance with."

Teresa makes a noise like biting on hard candy. "No, not the boys I dance with, but that's only where the people are, the teachers." Rosa nods, holds out her hand to touch Teresa's legs.

"Don't touch, it hurts. Listen to me, Rosa. This is a secret." Rosa really must concentrate. The pink comforter is no help. She bites down on her lip, tasting her own blood, hot and salty.

"Some boys don't listen when you're alone with them. Don't be alone with a boy."

"You have problems because you're pretty," Rosa says, touching her tongue, blotting at the blood with her finger. She and her sister both have dark eyes and hair, but Rosa's is cut short since she can't brush the tangles by herself. Rosa's face is defined by the same long eyebrows and oval face, yet it's stretched wide, making all her features larger than Teresa's. Rosa has larger breasts and thighs, too, a version of what Teresa might look like one day in middle age. Only the one leg has never grown into the shape of a woman.

"Oh Rosa, what did you do? Did you bite your tongue? Who told you that?" Teresa frowns, stroking the top of Rosa's head, blotting at her lip with the sponge.

"I heard Mamma and Papa say it about you. You get problems

when you have a pretty girl in a big city. I'm not pretty like you. No problems for me."

"Rosa, a boy might ask you to go alone with him sometime. You don't go. You understand?"

Rosa taps her foot. She can't imagine any boy asking her to go away with him, although there had been the boy who offered to walk her to the washroom at the dance. Miss Brown said he was a nice boy, and he was. He smelled like pine cones, and he took her to the bathroom upstairs, the far one, he said, because Rosa must like to have fun. Rosa giggled, said she did, and he put his hand on her blouse to fix her button. Rosa laughed, because he missed her button. Then the door opened, a young girl came out drying her hands against her yellow dress, and so she went in after and then he took her back to the dance. He hadn't asked her to go away with him. He hadn't asked her anything, not even her name. One day, Rosa knows, Teresa will go away. Go away with a boy, marry and have babies like their mamma.

"It's hot there, Tera?" Teresa nods. "I know," Rosa says, taking the tube of cream off Teresa's end table, "I'll put this on your legs and you'll feel better."

Rosa opens the bottle and squeezes the white liquid into a mound onto Teresa's sponge. Teresa stretches out her legs, and Rosa smells the flowers, but another smell, too, something Rosa can't make out, a strong smell, not very nice, maybe the smell of an animal, like her sister said, like the smell on your clothes when dogs get too close to you. Then she remembered walking one day with Teresa when a dog peed on the fence next door. Rosa laughed at the funny streak it made, and Teresa told her dogs do that to show where they've been. Now Rosa, too many images in her mind, is confused. Berries. Wolf. Boys. Trash. Dogs. She can't imagine everything together. Better to concentrate on Teresa's legs.

Cover Before Striking

"You smell nice, Tera," Rosa tells her, but Teresa isn't looking at her. Her face is covered with her arm and she curls herself up into a ball.

When Rosa goes back to bed, instead of looking at her picture book, she takes out her hairbrush and pretends to shave her legs until the bristles scratch her skin. "Look at me. I'm here," she says to the wolf and the girl in the red dress. Then she turns off the light, and thinks about her secrets.

Tear Stains: You're the only one who notices them.

The week before Magdala married all those years ago in Portugal, her mamma passed down her wedding dress and her mourning dress. Her own husband had been dead almost twelve years so she didn't need to wear the full black suit with the veil. She only needed to wear black. Magdala had been staring at the white frilly fabric, the delicately beaded cuffs and collar, wondering if the women had already altered the waist and the lace on her shoulders to suit her own figure when the black attire was thrown on top of her already full arms: an ankle-length starched skirt, a long billowy black knit blouse, and a short veil. "Every woman needs to prepare, Magda," her mamma told her. "My mamma did the same for me. She wore both of those. You're next." She hugged her daughter in rapture, the dresses collecting under Magdala's chin and bristling her ears, the black veil crossing her face like a net. She could barely see her mamma hunched over, arms wound tightly as string, pinching her ribs. As the smell of the bread rising in the kitchen mixed with the sting of the boiled onions and zucchini, mother and daughter thought of all the preparations that still had to get done before morning. Suddenly, they both started to cry.

Now Magdala sheds her tears on paper, the letters she receives from back home. News about the others, cousins she's never met, and her only sister, Maria, who stays home with her mamma. They try to keep in touch, offer news about the weather, gardens, weddings, or births, and Magdala smells each sheet of paper as it passes behind the next one, as if Portugal were contained in the neat lines and could be unzipped like a package. Then she carefully folds the papers, ties them with string, and adds them to the others neatly stored in the shoebox of her closet. She received another letter today, but won't read it until all the laundry is hung and she can retreat to the basement with a cup of hot tea.

As Magdala clips another white undershirt to the line, she wonders, not for the first time, why they decided on this house over twenty years ago. There were other houses made of brick on the same street, but they were red, not grey, and this house's driveway was clearly marked by two stone walls on each side of the entrance, two stone lions carved at the foot of the road. She wanted the house because of the privacy, the black gates around the front and back, and those grey walls. Now she wishes she had chosen one of the houses with a shared driveway or an open front yard where the children could have played ball or skipped and not run into gate or stone. But there was the issue of money. That's why they'd picked the Italian neighbourhood in Toronto instead of the Portuguese one. It was closer to Tonio's work and they didn't have a car. She thought it wouldn't matter since they were sending the children to English schools and teaching them bits of Portuguese around the house. But now Teresa knows more Italian than Portuguese, picked up from years of talking to other children and their parents on the street, and Rosa, well Rosa, when they realized what was wrong with her, they were thankful she would grow up in a neighbourhood where the children might tease her in a language she wouldn't understand. But Rosa too learned Italian. It was only Magdala who did not, and when she hangs her laundry, she can barely see the neighbours, let alone speak to them. Shaking out a wet sheet, Magdala tries to remember the last time she spoke a word outside the house or the grocery store, when she didn't just wave curiously over walls. Was it last summer? Last fall? Yes, it was last fall, when the Korean couple who run the corner store were robbed. A teenager in a ski mask hit the man over the head and asked for all the money. They called the police, Teresa told Magdala, but

Priscila Uppal

nothing could really be done about it, except that the Korean man had four stitches on his scalp. The next time Magdala went to buy a carton of milk, she'd said, "Sorry. So sorry to you and your wife." She felt like she was about to cry, and he looked confused, asked her if she needed help with something. "No. No. It's just good that you're in the neighbourhood," she said, but she knew she'd said everything wrong, should have made herself clear that she had heard about the robbery. Stunned to be talking to someone, Magdala could barely drop her change in to her purse and walk home.

There was another Portuguese family that lived down the street, beside the parkette, but they moved. They had an extra-large garden and even grew pumpkins in the fall. For a while, Magdala and the other woman exchanged vegetables, recipes, and sympathy cards, although they never went for walks or had tea unless there was a chore involved. Children and husbands had to come first. But it was nice to buy bread or compare fabric prices together, to speak the language of her mamma and her sister with someone besides Tonio. Then, ten years ago, when the last of the woman's children had left home, they moved to North York, and Magdala was alone once again.

Magdala misses her mother, although she would never write that in a letter. It's all right for her mother to say she misses her, and Madgala is sure the letter in her pocket will contain this declaration, but for Magdala to say she misses her mother means there is trouble in her marriage, and trouble in the marriage is never something to share with one's mother. These kinds of things are not to be discussed. Her mamma had outlived her husband already by a generation, and Magdala couldn't help wondering what her mamma thought about her own life, her own marriage, if she had planned to be with Papa forever, instead of her daughter, and was deeply pained, or if she was secretly relieved

Papa had died quickly and young, that she would never have to see him suffer or lose interest in her. These are things Magdala cries over, because it isn't right to ask. And it isn't right either to ask why Mamma had been so intent for Magdala to marry an older man, her senior by twenty years. But she knows why. Their village was dying. All the young men were moving to cities, to other countries to find work. Tonio had money, was kind, and was travelling to a better place, if a snowy one.

Oh, the snow! Madgala knows it's on its way. She can smell its crisp foreboding in the air. Only a few more weeks, maybe less, and she will no longer be able to hang her laundry outside, but will have to retreat into the basement to avoid all the falling leaves and frosts. *Mamma*, she thinks, staring up at all the billowing fabrics, *how I wish I had stayed with Mamma, laid in her arms a little longer, not taken away her dresses whether she wanted to get rid of them or not.* Soon Magdala will need the black dress. Tonio can't hold out much longer; it's only her constant care that has kept him alive for so long. The blood on the handkerchiefs spells his end, just as the first leaves on the ground spell the end of summer. The doctors are pessimistic about his chances. Yet he holds on lazily, and her hands bleach out the secret messages she can't write to her mother, can't tell her neighbours.

What happened to that Italian boy who used to work on the cars at all hours of the night? Magdala doesn't know, and she can't ask. Teresa had liked him, and Magdala had worried maybe they were sweet on each other. Too young. Too young. *My little Teresa must stay little forever, free of men, free of marriage, free of sickness and death*, she thought then. Now she sees a daughter full of life, full of prettiness, full of thoughts Magdala never had. What was it she said? She wanted to take courses in business? Maybe open a clothing store in the West End before the rents rise too high? Yes, that was it, but Magdala had stopped listening, imagining a boy in a ski mask hitting her over the head to get her money. "Better to get married," she told her. "Have someone buy you a house, make a vegetable garden." *Even that Italian boy would be all right*, she thought, *since he knows a trade.* And Teresa listened, or else she got herself into trouble first and listened later, but now there was a ring, she showed her the ring, and that other boy in the car was the man's cousin, yes, and she'd been dizzy because she'd fallen on the sidewalk, which is why he took her home. There was no need to get so upset and Papa wouldn't stop about his dreams, but everything is fine. He's Portuguese, too, but from Brazil. "Nice eyes, strong face and hands," Madgala told her daughter after shaking his hand for the first time. "A little dark, but that happens in Brazil. Everyone is mixed." Sheepishly, head bowed, Teresa said, "I will have to learn how to run a restaurant. He owns a restaurant, Mamma, with his brother. Maybe one day Rosa can help out, and we can open a clothing store, too." Magdala nodded happily, but wondered how much of it all was true. In the old days, Tonio would have gone out in the streets, asked around, met all the cousins and the rest of the family, but now Magdala just has to trust her daughter.

Once a year, Magdala bleaches the wedding dress to keep it fresh and white, make sure moths and mould don't have their way. Tough fabric, it has held for three generations and likely more if Teresa is careful when she has a daughter of her own. The long and simple skirt, straight cut with a thick circular line and laced at the waist, is probably back in style. The high neck and round pearl beads along the chest are elegant without being grand, the lace sash and cuffs symmetrical as butterfly wings. Wedding dress first, mourning dress afterward. Magdala is lucky, the first in three generations who hasn't lost her husband a decade before the first child reached adulthood. And Rosa will be here to take care of her when she starts to slip. Just like her

own sister and their mamma. Family tradition if one of the children is born that way. A curse on the child, but a blessing on the
mother since she will never be left alone. And Magdala needs
the help. Her back is already sore after only two loads of laundry.
There are still cucumbers and zucchini to chop, and she promised to teach Rosa cross-stitches this afternoon. The house will
need to be changed to suit her, Magdala reminds herself as the
wooden pins clip each thought to the clothes and sheets. Shelves
must be heightened, the garden properly marked, the bathroom
cupboards switched, and, of course, all the bedrooms must be
rearranged so Rosa can start to learn to take care of Magdala. It
won't be long after Papa that she ... she will need to teach Rosa.
Teach her things like what Magdala knows from the letters ...

... *the weather's hot. Mamma screams in her sleep. I worry.
She's old. She talks about Papa. She never used to. She talks about
her wedding and all the trips they were going to take before he
died. Hated her own mamma for not telling her about boys and
she was so scared when her belly started to grow. She drinks three
jugs of water a day and walks back and forth to the bathroom all
night....*

A wall of white in front of her, blocking everything else from
view, Magdala thinks of her wedding night in Portugal, how the
town had danced under the yellow lanterns her family had hung
from the trees, and Tonio, a few grey hairs across his temples,
had twirled her in his arms, called her his little girl. Leaning
against the bricks, another letter in her pocket, another load of
laundry hung, she wonders who will send sympathy cards, and
how they'll afford Teresa's wedding.

Wine Stains: Pour lots of salt onto the stain, dunk into cold water, and rub out.

Inside Tonio are two dreams: fire and water. His wife, Magdala, helps lift his large back away from the bed, holds him across the armpits to prop up his pillow, then slowly releases him. He recovers like a blade of grass. Looking out the window, he can see his undershirts and sheets on the line in the backyard, wooden pins marking the days he has survived in the trenches, all flags of white. "I surrender," he wants to tell his dreams. "I surrender." But still the shirts and sheets are hung.

Morning is roll call. Magdala peels off his shirt, throws it in her plastic basket. Then she pulls down the blankets, exposing legs limp like useless, splintered crutches, his olive skin wan and yellow without sun. She pats his thighs, meaning he should attempt to rise a little so she can slip off his underwear, flipping it quickly inside out and back again to examine it for stains. Into the same basket they go, whether or not there are any. A washed pair then appears, white cotton with an elastic waistband, a thin stripe of blue or black across the top. He doesn't watch, can't look down there without shaking. The only time he mentions it is if the band has caught on any hair.

This morning Tonio was dreaming before the sun hit his face. Shielding his eyes, he still saw Magdala opening the door, already dressed and working. "Papa," she said. "Time to get up." The sun denies him of his dreams, though he's been trying to embrace them, keep himself in the dream's arms so it will end. He wants to know how everything turns out, what happens after the fire and water rush over him. Magdala inspects the sheets for stains, tucking in stray sides as she does so, and leans in as she kisses him on the forehead to smell for sweat. This morning she doesn't need to change the sheets. Maybe later. She checks three times a day, more if he screams.

There are bombs inside Tonio's body: little bombs that go off randomly but persistently in twos or threes. Hot, hot, hot, they shoot up his arms and down his legs like burns, smelling like sulfur, stinging his nostrils. Tonio feels like he's had his hand on a hot stove for the last six years. And then there are the tides. Ones that swell inside his throat and want to rush out onto the bed, others that stir and churn inside his stomach as if a drain were plugged. They steam inside him, pound against his veins, pour out of his body. Every entry a spout. "Move on," he tells the tides. "Keep marching and you'll overtake them." Tonio knows the tides and the bombs are a part of him, and yet they are also enemies, trying to silence him, making it difficult for him to speak his words or tell his dreams.. They don't want to be detected. Masters of camouflage.

"There are bombs, Magda." He wants to tell her more, but the small dish is in front of him and Magdala has put a plastic spoon in his right hand.

"The war is over, Tony. You're at home." She walks over to the window on the left side of his bed and opens the blinds. The sun rushes against her face, turning her into an outline. Tonio would rather the blinds were shut. It's harder to fall asleep in the afternoons with the sun in his face and his eyes are too sore to read anymore. Because the blinds are cracked, even when shut the few missing rungs allow for light and the sight of his laundry waving in the breeze, his empty shirt sleeves helpless.

Tonio slams his hand down on the bed, trying to pound out his words. He starts to cough and Magdala rubs his back, procures a handkerchief, and holds it in front of his mouth to catch the spit. "The doctor is coming tomorrow, Papa." He shakes his head and coughs harder. Magdala rests her basket, sighing as her body relieves itself of the burden of the weight, and calmly waits for the fit to pass. Sometimes she hums, trying to soothe him, or, if his eyes are open, smiles to show him she's not worried. He tries to focus on the photographs hung on the right wall, pictures of the girls and Magdala when she was younger, recently arrived in Toronto, in front of the new house. Tonio, with hand gestures and broken English, had asked one of the neighbours, now he can't remember which, to take the photograph for them. The camera was also new. It was a time of new things. Rosa would be born in less than a year. Teresa three years later.

"No more doc —" Two bombs explode up Tonio's arms. His head slams against Madgala. She holds her face, biting her lip to hold in the pain. "Okay, Tony," she says. "No more doctors. It's easier on the children."

Tonio's fire abates and he hands her back the damp handkerchief. She throws it in the basket and places a white one on the nightstand. He feels small in the room, in the king-size bed, as if he's been shrinking. He remembers when he was first brought in here, for good, he was sure the room didn't have enough air, that he wouldn't be able to get used to the cramped space. But, over the years, the room has become a whole land, a settler's field he has lost the strength to plough, and he anticipates that soon he will be reaped, shucked into a wooden barrel, and delivered elsewhere. He starts to eat, the hot porridge massaging his gums. Magdala leaves the room, closing the door behind her.

One day Tonio might like to sleep with the window open, maybe dream about wind, but he can't reach. The one time he tried, Magdala caught him, screamed, and he lost his balance and fell on the floor. It took both girls to lift him back on the bed. "Don't move, Papa. You could hurt yourself," they warned him.

He asked, "What do I do if there's a fire?"

"There's no fire, Papa," they said.

He tried to tell them, waving his fingers frantically through the air in circles like smoke.

"Hold his hands down," Magdala told the girls. "He might hit himself." And they obeyed, strapping him down on the bed, unaware of his melting skin.

Tonio can hear the rumble of the washing machine through the vents, its starts and stops, the regular burbling of the wash cycle. He imagines his clothes, their stains, drowning in the water, spitting out into the basin. Before, they had talked about moving him to the basement. Fewer stairs, and Magdala spent most of her day down there doing chores. They could be closer. She could reach him earlier if needed. And he would have a window at ground level to call her when she was outside. "We could make it nice, Tony. I could hire someone to move all the furniture and put down a carpet."

He protested. "Too much work for you, Mamma. You have enough to do already." But there were days he wished he would wake up and find himself down there in the basement, listening to the washing machine, dreaming of thunder and hot rains and bleached white sheets spinning.

In many of his dreams, Tonio's crawling in the garden, pushing down the lines of wooden stakes with his arthritic hands, his feet dragging behind in the dirt like heavy luggage. He can hear the push of the water and smell the pull of the smoke; this is when the dreams combine. To his left are all the fabrics hung on the line, motionless without wind, necklines drooped like people in prayer. The endless days he struggles in and out of those lines stand erect. "I surrender," he tries to say, but can't get the words out; he tries, but has to keep his mouth shut against the smoke, his eyebrows starting to burn. He can feel each individual hair parting. The neighbours, the ones he remembers from years ago, the Italian couple with the large van and the

three boys, yes, it was the man who had taken the photograph
for them the day they moved in, are in their backyard, drinking
or walking, the boys playing ball or running under a sprinkler,
yelling in English mixed with Italian. He can barely understand
either, but he knows basic words. "Water!" he yells, but no one
hears him. They are busy playing and talking, and no one sees
him crawling on the ground. The last time he had the dream, he
got farther and started to dig in the garden with his hands, pulling up cold, black soil. *Maybe if I plant myself upside down and
perfectly straight, like a carrot*, he thought, *it will all be over*.
He would have figured it out. He had been digging, holding his
breath to keep out the elements, when the sun peeled open his
eyes this morning.

Magdala returns with a letter, places it on his nightstand
beside the handkerchief, smiling, her cheeks cracked with deep
lines. "A letter, Papa, from Portugal. I'll read it to you later."
Tonio nods, pleased to see her smiling, the ribbons of white hair
twirled into a bun, reminding him of the flowers she wore on
their wedding day.

"You're such a good woman, Magda." She pauses to scan
his face, then kisses his forehead. Tonio feels sealed by her lips,
to be opened later when she has the time to sit and love him.
He knows she skips parts of the letters, probably when they ask
about his health. He can tell. She pretends she can't make out
the handwriting, that, out of practice, it takes her longer each
time to make out the Portuguese, and then she flips the page
behind the envelope. Sometimes she says, "Oh, this part isn't
interesting to you. It's just a recipe." Sometimes she says nothing and hides her eyes.

"You should send your recipe for stains," he tells her, nodding his head vigorously as he usually does when he praises her.
"They always come out." When the laundry comes back, he is

often amazed by the clean slate in front of him, tells himself today, today, there will be no need for any more. Today they will stay white ...

Tonio wakes again to Magdala's voice rolling across her tongue and teeth like waves in their old speech, the letter held up in front of her reading glasses. "... the weather's hot ... Mamma ... drinks three jugs of water a day and goes back and forth to the washroom all night ... isn't that funny, Tony?"

He nods, gives her a little chuckle, and sips the glass of wine she brought him, content she let him have some in the afternoon to help him sleep. He tries to make it last, hoping if he takes his time it won't flood his body, but already he can feel his toes filling up with fluid. He wants to tell his wife about the water dreams, how the water spreads over him like a thick wet blanket and he sinks. Wants to tell her how it feels not to breathe anymore. He wonders what her mamma dreams of, if she tells her daughter, if that is the part she skipped over in the letter. Tonio has never met anyone underneath the water in his dreams before, but maybe he hasn't been looking. Maybe they could meet, touch hands, get out of the dream together.

"What a big garden they have again back home," Magdala says, eyeglasses on her lap, face turned towards the window.

"You make the best zucchini."

"It's been a good year, Papa," she sighs. "They grew big and firm. Maybe next year will be a good year, too."

"You did it, Magda." Tonio nods vigorously and starts coughing. Magdala jumps off her stool and shoves the letter and envelope into the pocket of her apron. Silent, she hands over a fresh handkerchief, waits to see how bad the fit will be, then walks to the other side of the bed to shut the blinds, the missing slats like empty spaces in an old smile.

"I was crawling in the dirt and ..."

"Tony, the war is over."

No, he tries to tell her, no, no. He can't get it out; only the coughs. The fire swells in his lungs. Tonio wants to build himself a shelter in the garden, beside the zucchini, the firm and large vessels almost as tall as the stakes, wants to become one of them, wrapped in tough wax, plucked ripe. He has a plan, wants to tell Magdala he has a plan, if only he could just finish his dream uninterrupted. If only he could have wind, maybe the sheets would move and someone would see he has already surrendered. When things move, people notice them, he thinks. Let me dig my hole.

Magdala picks up the plastic meal tray and turns to leave. "You need anything, Papa?"

"A hole in the dirt."

Madgala stops at the door, her back to Tonio. "Don't say that Tony, please ..." She closes it behind her.

Tonio wants to see the girls today, but knows that he won't. He said too much and said it all wrong, and he curses the dreams that keep his words away, hoarding them, shoving them deeper inside his body. *The little bombs are like my words,* he thinks, *shooting inside all hot, fiery, and useless, poking me in the ribs and thighs, making me feel but not tell.* Rosa and Teresa. He wants to see them. They are good girls to their papa, but Teresa's too pretty and Rosa knows about the dreams. He can tell. She dreams, too, but he doesn't know what she dreams of, and neither of them could ever find the right words to share them. She always says, "Sweet dreams, Papa. Sweet ones today," and Tonio wants to take her in his arms and kiss her, even though she is too big, and sometimes he can't control his hands so the girls aren't supposed to touch him in case they get hit. So, instead, they wave to each other, nod, and once in a while Rosa combs his hair. Tonio tells Magdala what to say to them, especially if he thinks they're in trouble. He tells her to warn Teresa about boys and Rosa about crossing the street. "Teach Rosa how to do things for herself," he says. "Soon you'll need her." And Magdala has been teaching her all about the chores. She's a good woman. She knows about these things.

Tonio never sees the girls in the dreams, but thinks that sometimes they can see him from the window. Maybe they want to see what he'll do, if he can make it, and when he thinks this, he can feel their eyes on him like rays. Sometimes the girls hang the shirts on the line for their mamma. They help out, see the stains, wash them out. All have been passed the recipe. They know the things he can't help doing. Know about the laundry. Some days he can smell the sting of all that salt as they pass by his door. But he doesn't see their hands in his dreams, rubbing out his shirts and sheets, cold under the water. The hands that need to work are his own. He is the one in charge of getting out.

Good shirts, all white and strong, no holes. Tonio holds on to the one he is wearing, stripping the front off his wine-sweaty chest, crunching his hands into fists. Pulling, rocking on the bed, he tries to rip it. The top, he notices, has a stronger stitch than the bottom, so he switches his mode of attack, yanking the cloth down and up, until his fingernails hurt and he can't catch his breath. The shirt is swollen but undefeated, and he is coughing hard again. Rosa knocks. By the height of the sound, he can tell that she is using her leg to hit against the wood.

"Papa? Papa? You need Mamma?"

He waves her away, but the door is between them. Alone. He wants to be alone. Alone with his white shirt. But he can hear Rosa's uneven walk shuffling down the hallway, and soon she is calling for Mamma, Mamma. Magdala charges in, shutting the door on Rosa.

Tonio starts to cry.

"Have you had an accident? Don't cry, Papa. I can wash the sheets." Nodding, he lets her lift his frame, bend him, and turn him sideways until all the corners of the sheets are untucked. Then a hard tug and a quick smell, her nose like a small animal's. Opening the door, she then hands the sheets to Rosa, the white middle stained yellow, the left corner red. Rosa trudges downstairs and Tonio knows she will start the rigourous rubbing before placing the sheets in the washer. He also knows he won't be given any more wine to sip.

Tonio holds out his arm. He wants to touch Magdala, tell her everything is fine, that she doesn't understand, the dream will end soon. Wants to feel her strong cheeks, bury himself in the grey ribbons of her hair. She walks over, kisses him on the forehead, wipes away her own sweat underneath her nose. Upset that he has failed to keep everything white once again, he turns his head on his pillow and pretends to fall asleep. Magdala gives the rest of the room a quick inspection, checks the wastebasket, then the four corners, lingering for a moment on the photographs on the wall as if deciding whether or not to move them, then exits, shutting the door. Tonio stares out the cracked blinds to the garden, wonders where all the fire and water will go, what they will take with them. One day, perhaps soon, in his fits of coughing, he'll know, and rid himself of both dreams.

Rust Stains: Apply lemon juice and salt; then place in oven.

She is surprised it hasn't died yet. Endlessly, every day, it turns and turns; then rests its weary frame at night, though it seems to be on its last legs, moaning and trudging along, wide torso churning.

Having insisted on helping with the wash, Teresa waits for the spin cycle to stop. With Mamma's back trouble it's getting difficult for her to carry the loads herself, even if the stairs are few to the basement. Soaking in salt in the metal basin are Papa's sheets, turning the white water pink. She will scrub them with more detergent before inserting them in the next load. Soon the wash will be entirely Rosa's job, when Teresa marries and leaves the house, although this will not happen before Papa dies. But she has her ring, her promise, her simple silver band and four-karat diamond, in the bottom drawer of her dresser, in the pocket of her good pair of black pants that she wears only to funerals. Until she wears those pants to bid Papa a final goodbye, it helps him to have his girls in the house.

She showed Mamma the ring a month ago, two weeks after Wilhelm proposed, when they were out drying the laundry. But she hasn't shown Papa the ring, or Rosa. Rosa wouldn't be able to keep her mouth shut, they decided, and Papa still likes to think of the girls as the little children they were when he was first confined to the bedroom. No one wants to upset Papa. Mamma does the dirty work, dumping the pan if Papa is able to warn her in time, or else cleaning his underwear. Lifting his frame, she arranges him into positions for eating and sleeping, and reads letters from back home out loud to him until they are both choked up and Papa coughing. There is blood sometimes, too, that Mamma tries to hide. Teresa worries about where the blood comes from, which part of Papa hurts the most. At first she thought it was blood on Papa's sheet, like on the clothes she threw away, and she was prepared to throw out Papa's sheets, too. However, upon closer inspection, the sweet linger of the smell informed her otherwise. So, she filled the basin with hot water and now watches it swoosh in waves beside the rumble of the machine.

When Teresa is alone in her room, she likes to hold the engagement ring in her hand, but then returns it guiltily to the darkness of her drawers when she hears Papa's coughing. No dreaming yet of what is to come. Not that she's anxious to leave exactly either. Wilhelm is a nice man, it's not that. And handsome. They met at his restaurant, House of Rio, a diner where she and her friends sometimes stopped for coffee and cake after school. Wilhelm was washing the countertops and offered her an extra slice of carrot cake. Then he started picking her up from school. Lots of her friends knew about it, about her romance with this man almost ten years older, and then a man at the restaurant, a regular customer — the one she won't name anymore — offered her a lift. She agreed, but he didn't take her home, not right away, and she was scared and tried to fight him but … and Mamma saw her get out of the …Wilhelm is a nice man. He has gentle brown eyes and hairy arms and his hands are tender, even comforting on her neck and shoulders, or up and down her legs. He promises to help her open a store, promises to help Rosa. Her friends are excited that she will be the first among them to get married. One even said it's smart of her to get out of the whole college and university mess by plunking herself right into a family business. And maybe it is, though it's weird to think that many of her friends will be in school when she's married and washing restaurant dishes, chopping vegetables, buying cakes, and then, later, having babies. How will she be able to do the things in the restaurant or her store plus all the things Mamma does: cleaning, cooking, changing, gardening? For now, at least, she is just the helper with the wash, her papa's little girl.

"Good girl," Mamma said when Teresa produced the silver ring with the small diamond, warm from clutching it tightly in her pocket. "Just make sure you're not showing before the wedding."

"Mamma! I'm not pregnant."

Mamma looked surprised, but obviously believed her, the expression on her face changing from stern practicality to a wan hope.

"Then we can wait, Tera?"

Teresa agreed.

And Teresa can wait, too, wait as long as she has that ring tucked away: her promise. Wilhelm won't betray her. She visits him every day at the restaurant, and he is, by all accounts, a man in love. "Family first," he said, when she told him about waiting for Papa. "So many young people don't understand that anymore. I'm glad you do." Now she can still go to school, to the dances, shopping with friends, and take Rosa to the park or help her with sewing. And she knows her mother is happy she won't be going to college or university to make a career for herself. "Girls are silly to want to act like men. They have no idea what men go through. The wars," Mamma told her, "the wars could happen again, and then who will watch out for the children?" Teresa likes some of the old ways. Yes, she likes the idea of marriage and doesn't want to be one of *those* girls, but there are also so many rules: the rule that makes Rosa stay in the house and take care of Mamma after Papa dies, the rule that Mamma can't put Papa in a hospital, the rules about babies, the many babies she will be expected to have, unless she has one like Rosa.

When Teresa dreams about the wedding, she dreams about

how everyone will dance, even Rosa, and the machinations behind her turn into music, the soaked sheet into a massive tablecloth. Mamma will smile, clap her hands, and grab on to a chair, thinking Papa beside her. Then a tall white cake rises to the front of her mind, along with frilly decorations, and proud invitations, especially the ones to Mamma and Papa's families back in Portugal who won't be able to come. Her hair will be worn up, in a twist, and she'll carry white lilies in her hands. Sure, they will have to skimp on a few things, there has never been a lot of money and Wilhelm wants to put money aside for the future clothing store, but traditions are still traditions and the nice thing is she knows she will have all the necessities no matter what happens. Mamma says so and when Papa is gone …

"Look, Tera!"

Shaking herself from her dream, Teresa pulls off her rubber laundry gloves. Rosa offers up a skirt for her inspection, a green paisley pattern with wide swirls that Teresa recognizes as the old coarse fabric from the basement curtains.

"Look at the stitches, Tera!"

Teresa examines the cloth, turning it over and inside out. The stitches are firm when she tugs. Obviously nervous, humming to herself and tapping her good leg, Rosa beams when the stitches hold.

"Very good. Really good," Teresa tells her, the spin cycle rolling on behind them, and it is. Rosa is good with her hands, learns quickly if you show her exactly how. There are times Teresa thinks that Rosa has the most talent, and could make a wonderful wife, if she just wasn't the way she is. In a certain light, Rosa appears almost grandmotherly, her thighs loose like after childbearing, her breasts down to her stomach if she isn't wearing a bra. It makes Teresa wonder what kind of children she will have, if she might resemble Rosa more afterwards.

"I made it for you to dance in. Put it on."

Smiling, Teresa slips the skirt over her pants. Rosa's firm hands zip it up in the back. The skirt is a little formless for Teresa's taste, and the pattern is faded lime in a couple of spots, but it fits and rests pleasantly at the knee.

"Thanks, Rosa," Teresa says, taking it off and placing it in the laundry basket she will use later to carry the clean clothes.

Rosa sways her arms and pounds her foot on the ground to the thumping of the washing machine until the strap on her brace comes off. Grimacing, Rosa bends down to fix it, the canvas strip tight in her fist like rope.

"I'm not too good at dancing."

"Sure you are, Rosa. You'll dance soon."

When Rosa has retied the strap securely, Teresa picks up some wooden pins. "You did a fine job, Rosa. Now Mamma could use some help outside."

Rosa accepts the pins as they drop into her hand. Teresa waves her on and Rosa obeys. Mamma's worn running shoes pass by the window.

The washer goes into a fit, the little shelf holding the cleaners suffering a tiny earthquake. But Teresa knows the routine. It always does this moments before resting. Coughing and spitting up water, banging against the concrete wall, it sweats itself dry. Then there's the silence that means it's all over. But this time, when the silence arrives, Teresa abandons her dreaming and runs upstairs to check on Papa.

The Boy Next Door

If I told you my mother ran away with the boy next door, I wouldn't be lying. Except that he was a man, not a boy. And a priest, not my father. But he did live next door. And my mother did run away with him. Although it was more like walking, very calmly, an organized exodus.

I had thought my mother's keen interest in church was a direction of her energies toward my soul. My first confession was coming up in the next few months and as with any big Catholic event I believed she wanted to make sure I would perform it properly in front of the neighbourhood. She had been a regular churchgoer before then and wrote for *Our Faith*, the church bulletin, articles about bake sales and ads for seniors who were looking for companions to take them grocery shopping. She wrote her pieces at night, pulling out the extension of the dining-room table, laying her typewriter on top. She was a valued member of the congregation and we attended every Sunday, sprinkling ourselves with holy water and kneeling on the smooth pine floor. Then, over the course of that spring, she started to take on extra parish duties: helping clean the pews, baking cookies for the prayer group and the choir, passing out flyers, and arranging rummage sales. She didn't seem to pray more that I knew, but she started spending more time in church than at home. I assumed Father Marcus approved of her as a good neighbour, or concluded that she had felt the good grace of God between the hedges separating our houses from one another.

Father Marcus was not the pastor. That was Father Brown. He had been the main pastor at Resurrection for thirty years and was well-liked by the parishioners, especially the older ones, who seemed to see him as a direct link to the heavens. The other priest had only been preaching for two years before he left for another town, to be closer to his family we were told. His job was to take over the lighter times of worship and help the children at my school with catechism. Father Marcus replaced him and moved next door because Father Brown liked living in the church. He had gotten used to it, though a church widow had died and left her house for him. That's how the story goes and how he came to live beside us. I didn't mind. He was young and seemed nice, and he countered Father Brown's solemn hymns, like "The Lord is My Shepherd" and "Lamb of God," which we would sing as if our throats were made of shame, with lively psalms of joy like "He is the One" and "We Are the Children." Sometimes I had to restrain myself from clapping as I sang these new songs, and besides, he wore only his collar and would play murder ball with the boys at recess and hopscotch with the girls. He spent a lot of time outside, his skin tanned and taut, his legs flexible for the sports, with hair dark and even without a touch of grey. Before school, if he was around, he would turn the end of my skipping rope on the driveway so I could jump if none of my friends were outside. He had even learned some of our songs, "Steamboat Sally" and the "Big Bad Wolf," and his strong voice slammed down with every slap of the rope on tar. He carried home lots of food, plastic bags hanging like extensions from his body. Loved to cook. If our kitchen window was open we could smell his peppers and tomatoes, chicken and beef, frying or steaming, turning colour. After Communion, which tasted exactly the same to me as biting the rim off a Styrofoam cup, was the only time the church was full of food. Mostly sweets, cakes and tarts and watery tea I would sip while waiting for my mother. The smell of the church basement snacking was sterile, nothing like the aroma from next door that stung the eyes and rose in the air, inviting.

Once confession lessons started, it was another story. I tried to think of what sins I could tell Father Marcus, and every time I saw him I was reminded of the secrets he would know about me. I played farther away from the house, thinking God was too close to my thoughts before I could work them out, figure out how to explain them properly. He could watch my whole family from his backyard while we swam or barbecued or he worked on his vegetable garden, his legs bending like grass, straight-edged and graceful, pulling up carrots and cucumbers in his gloved hands. He wore white shorts on truly hot days, and I was amazed by the thick dark hair that curled all over his legs, forming a kind of coat around him, making his almost black eyes seem even more piercing. I wondered if he was keeping tabs on sins I didn't remember, some commandment I had violated like not honouring my father and mother, or lying. I wanted to ask him if some sins were more forgivable than others, or whether there were any sins that couldn't be forgiven. On a tour of the confessionals, those boxes painted like small houses and without the stained-glass pictures as on the rest of the church, I noticed the screen was thin like the one on our gazebo. I could tell it was Father Marcus, so I'm sure he could tell it was me inside. I wanted to change what he knew about me, imagining what joy there could be in shocking him, repeating dirty words or telling him I sometimes wished my parents were dead. I felt tantalized at the whim of hearing him gasp, afraid for a moment of the girl next door who skipped in the mornings, that he could think I was dangerous.

At the same time, I had begun to find out about kissing. I knew about it already, seen my mom kiss my dad quickly on the lips, watched longer full-mouthed kisses on television, but had never felt what the fuss was about. You would need to confess kissing at my age, I knew. God did not approve of us kissing, but at recess we would sneak behind the monkey bars to the brick wall and play a game. You would ask for a kiss, and then everyone else would choose who was supposed to kiss you. You would close your eyes and wait until they had decided. Silently, someone would approach, the heat of their mouth close as the silence of expectation rose, and press down. The rule was you couldn't open your eyes and couldn't tell who had been delegated with the role of kisser, but we did, of course. And some kisses were better than others, I understood that, and sometimes they weren't from the boy you liked.

The kissing game had been a source of prayer for me. I asked God to forgive my lips of their sins and to wash me clean before I went to bed at night. I would tell Him I promised to try my best not to do it again until I was older. I would shiver, imagining the dark booth of the confessional awaiting the secrets of all those backdoor kisses in the broad daylight, where anyone who went behind the wall could have witnessed the game. My mom had put me in the choir and I would sing "Ave Maria" and "Blessed Be the Lord" in the front row, my clean, pressed, white dress covering my body to my toes, and think of that brick wall that smelled of urine and bubble gum, wondering if the altar boys (some who I knew) would tell Father Marcus or Father Brown about the one time I let them look up my dress on a dare. I would

blush all through Mass, trying not to look any of the parishioners in the face. I kept my eyes glued to the arched ceiling as the
blinding light floated down upon our heads. My father said he
thought I had a little crush on Father Marcus. I told him it was
on God.

In school we listened to lectures on baptism and Christ's
death, tales of thorns and nails, hunger and rotten kisses. *If He
had already died for our sins, what was the point of confessing?* I
wanted to ask. But no one asked questions in class. We took notes
and stared at the crucifix nailed to the border of the blackboard.
A naked man we were supposed to love spread for all of us to
see. It was after class that I could sometimes dig up the nerve
to ask questions. Especially if I was sitting outside and Father
Marcus happened to pass by and ask how I was, then I would
have something ready for him to clarify, like why Peter falling
asleep was such a bad thing, or how come Mary was God's bride
and not Jesus's mother? He would sit down with me on the concrete steps, his dark eyebrows raised in earnest, and explain. I
wondered about Christ up on that cross, and what people had
wanted from him.

"Why did they have to kill him naked?" I asked, tentative
about saying the word naked to a priest.

"They wanted to humiliate him," Father Marcus replied.

"Oh."

"You seem confused."

"I thought maybe they were curious," I whispered.

Father Marcus stroked his collar with his fingers. "Maybe
they were. Israel is a very hot country."

I made a habit of going next door without asking. Father Marcus
was always willing to receive me, even if he was cooking. I would

help him chop zucchini, or slice crumbly white cheese we didn't have at home, and he would sing hymns or teach me recipes; how long to boil the water, how to know how much paprika to add. He could even make roses out of radishes, his fingers quick and selective, and I would write some of his lessons down on a pad of yellow paper he kept by the phone. He told me my mother would appreciate it. She and my father would eat the new dishes (if we were missing a mysteriously spelled spice, Father Marcus would provide it in a tiny plastic bag) and my father would read his newspaper at the table, mumbling between chewings how good my mom could cook. Later the hot spices would send him up to bed to toss and turn in his blankets or hold his cramping belly in the bathroom. Then he said they gave him bad dreams, never had the stomach for foreign cooking. The meals had strange names, Portuguese names I didn't know how to pronounce, from Brazil, where Father Marcus came from. One day I found Brazil on the map pinned to our classroom bulletin board. Although it wasn't as large as Canada, I was sure it contained many more spices. I would flail my hands around my mouth from the heat at first, but gradually, with practice, I could place the spices directly onto my tongue without flinching.

I had been practising the harmony section of "The Lord Is My Shepherd" when I noticed the forgotten casserole my mom had baked for Father Marcus. She had spent all day in the kitchen breaking eggs and soaking vegetables, pushing me gently into other rooms to practise without disturbing her. I clasped the heavy dish in my hands, raking in the smell of sweet tomatoes, zucchini, and beef, and strolled up his stairs. I noticed the door was slightly ajar and cupped my sole around it, kicking back a little. I wandered through his living room where black-and-white pictures of dark-haired people in light clothes hung alongside coloured paintings of the Virgin and Jesus. I had pointed to those pictures on one occasion and asked him who they were. He said he didn't know, that they were just decoration, and he looked a little sad, his lips curling around the edges. I was on my way to the kitchen when I saw my mother collapsed in the arms of Father Marcus, giving him a TV kiss, a long one, part of her yellow silk blouse hanging off her shoulder, her light brown hair curled around her neck, her lips an offering. I nearly dropped the casserole, and then clung on to it like a stuffed animal, biting the Saran Wrap. Father Marcus opened his eyes and saw me there. He didn't even flinch, closing one eye, his mouth moving toward her neck, and I was glad that my mother never turned around. I sneaked out the door, casserole in hand, shaking. He caught me before I could get through my own front door.

"Come here," he said calmly, his heavy-lidded eyes downcast.

I couldn't disobey a priest, but I wanted to. I was going to cry and didn't want him to know. When I looked at his face I saw my mother's lips pressing on him, the same lips that she would blot thick with "kissing-red" lipstick, as a joke, because I loved the name, and smack my cheeks. He took the casserole out of my hands, had to give a forceful tug on it if I remember correctly, and laid it on the bottom stair like a loose brick. I had already started to cry, turning away from him, wrapping my arms around my stomach.

"It's all right. Don't worry."

He was reaching out his hand for me to hold, but I put mine behind my back, even though I wanted to wipe my face free of the tears.

"You saw us, didn't you, dear."

I nodded.

"Me and your mom."

I nodded again and kicked at the stone stairs.

"It's natural for your mom and I to kiss. We love each other, you see."

I knew priests were supposed to love everyone, but the thought of my mother's arms wrapped around him, touching his body. His body.

"I didn't know priests had lips!" I yelped and slid around his legs on the steps, heaving, trying to take in enough air to keep listening.

"Priests have a lot of things," he said. "We're just like other people."

"No you're not." That I was sure of.

"Not entirely … we cook better."

I pressed my face against his chest for a moment and he went in to get me a washcloth.

That night I ran straight up to my room and faked a stomach ache so as not to eat dinner with my mom and dad. My dad just accepted it and didn't come up to check on me, his spoon already dug deep into another casserole. My mother did. I don't think Father Marcus told her what I saw, but she came to tell me that in a couple days we would be leaving when my father left for work. We were going to fly in a plane and have a vacation. I started to cry again. She brought me ginger ale for my tummy, and told me we would all be happy, and not to tell Dad. That wasn't difficult.

On the Tuesday we packed quickly, just as she said we would, right after Dad left for work. We took only "necessities," as she called them, and "favourites." For me this included a few clothes, a red-haired beanbag doll I'd had since I was a baby, and a toothbrush. My mother also took very little, her purse and some clothes, saying we would buy new things, but that night she had been up late typing her last letter for the church bulletin and I figured she didn't pack because she was pretty tired. On a yellow piece of paper I wrote "*I'll miss you*" and shoved it in my father's sock drawer at the bottom. He never really liked to travel.

Father Marcus arrived with two suitcases and passports for all of us. A week earlier, as a surprise, my mom had taken me to a photo booth and the same black-and-white picture was staring at me in the tiny book. We took a taxi to the airport and Mom bought me a teen magazine to read on the trip. I asked her if Dad was sad and she gave me a pill that she said would soothe my stomach. I asked Father Marcus why he wasn't wearing his collar, and he said it was easier to get through Customs that way. I don't remember much else. I was fast asleep before we even boarded.

When we got off the plane, Mom told me we were in Brazil, the land of spices I pointed to on a map. It was so dry and hot that I asked if there was a pool. She said there was an ocean. We arrived in a town called Biguaçu, and a man with a thick-tongued accent took our few bags up a walkway, and we entered a brick house, the side toward the sun a shade lighter than the rest, at the end of a solitary street with a white swing outside. I loved the place as soon as we walked in. It smelled of Father Marcus's cooking.

It took my dad three days to discover we were gone. Sometimes my mother would leave dishes on the stove for my father to heat up, or he would order takeout if she was busy at church. With the upcoming first confessions, he thought she would be spending most of her time there. He only noticed on the Sunday when he went to Resurrection and didn't see her or me in the choir. My mom told me this after she talked to him for the first time. He had called the police.

On the fridge was the church bulletin, held up with alphabet magnets like one of my pictures or report cards. He found it on the Sunday and searched it for a mother-daughter retreat or other function he hadn't heard about. He read the whole thing three times and handed it to the officers as possible places to look for us. They asked him some questions, told him that Father Marcus had also disappeared, and that maybe finding one would help them to find the others. My father offered them some beer and they read the bulletin together. Under "Obituaries and Announcements" was my mother's short and sweet article: "Rebecca Creely has moved on to greener pastures. She leaves behind her husband and asks him not to worry." One of the policemen pointed it out. My father hadn't noticed. She had used her maiden name.

Apparently he continued on fairly normally. Except for the chuckles when he walked by, my father's routine didn't change at all. He called me after a couple weeks, or I should say I did, and I told him that we were happy here. He said he was happy. I asked him if he was eating okay. He answered that the church was sending him food for the next while; he was well taken care of and had so many casseroles and cookies he would probably have to throw some to the birds. I told him I loved him. He said he was going to read the paper.

One of the women who baked for my father was a widow. Her husband had died in a car accident or something. They don't talk about it much. She and my father were married within two years and the chuckles lessened. They were joined together by Father Brown one year before he retired. They replaced the other priest with a Canadian. My father calls and asks me the same questions he did six years ago. I tell him I skip rope and love to sing. I tell him I go to church.

None of us do. We still pray, but don't go to church. I have a stepbrother from a previous marriage of Father Marcus's. His name is Brio and he has the room beside me. We are learning how to cook together and go to the same school. I have let him touch my breasts the way we are taught to hold tomatoes under the tap. I know I should stop this, I'm only fifteen, but I don't know if I can stop myself, and here, I don't have to go to confession.

Wind Chimes

My father, my uncle and I, and two cousins who still lived in town, one nephew barely a man, carried the coffin down the main road to the Anglican graveyard. The plain oak casket, void of wreaths save a white rosebud cluster on each end, seemed too light on my shoulders. Though she wasn't a heavy woman, she trod on the ground as if she were, and I fought back the urge to check inside the closed hatch to make sure she was actually dead. That night I woke my wife in tears and told her my mother was trapped, suffocating with stray cats and little boys twisted in car crashes — all buried alive, and I was supposed to be among them. A fever of 102 degrees, my wife informed me later. I shook as if caught in a bitter wind.

Though my mother wasn't an Anglican, she'd remarked frequently on the beauty of the dark iron gate and the white oaks sheltering the local Anglican church's graveyard, so my father thought it would be the best resting place for her. But she belonged to a different religion and was a congregation of one before I was born and became her disciple. She collected wind chimes. Dozens of wind chimes hung along the eavestroughs of our roof, clanging against each other. Some stayed up all year and some, frequently depending on colour, were reserved for particular seasons: rich orange and bright yellow for autumn, metals like steel or silver for winter, mauves and blues for spring, and whites or pinks for summer. The chimes all had secret hidden names, my mother claimed, names she couldn't divulge to me out of respect, though I often asked her and she seemed pleased, tousling my hair or pinching my side playfully, when I tried to guess, offering up everything from Sally and Larry to Honey-Eyes or Acorn-Breath or Bee-Beauty. If you listen, she said, they will sing to you. You will understand. My mother believed death was twofold. "Two tunes for each soul," she instructed. "One is for us and one is for the dead. Only they can hear that one." The wind chimes' songs filled me with a distant, unreachable ache, bearable only because she was beside me, my head in her lap on the porch.

Dead was a word I could understand, since I could spell it and use it in conversation. Uncle Billy is dead. Grandma Barnes and Great-Aunt Elisabeth are dead. But the first death I ever witnessed was the death of our dog. The collie, a stray that had latched on to our family before I was born, had no official name, just "Girl." My mother said we didn't need to name her, or put her on a leash. "Just as she was free to come, she must be free to leave." Secretly, I called her Raisin, because she loved to eat raisins from my hands. When she got hit by the truck, I was astonished at how quick death was, how ordinary.

I watched my father from the driveway, a large man who moved slowly, kicking grey pebbles onto the street, the line between the beginning of the road and the place of death, a line of black tar I refused to cross. Raisin had been split open from her neck down to her tail by the impact of the front wheels. Her fur was matted with blood, her nose crushed to the point of disappearance. Incisors sliced through her cheeks. The trail of blood testified she had travelled several feet. She was worse than lifeless to me; she was shameful, punctured with tar and dirt, a damp banana peel, probably from the truck's wheels, smashed across her stomach. Her body smelled like rotten milk. I counted three legs. Father scraped her up with a shovel into a trash bag, and carried her into Corner's Field, a mile west from our home. I hoped the neighbours weren't watching.

A silent man in general, my father's silence during this affair was typical, unlike my mother, who could be heard wherever you happened to be in the house, humming and making rhythms with her hands on tabletops or feet on foot boards, swinging pots and pans, or ringing the small gold antique bell in the living room that she inherited from Great-Aunt Elisabeth. For my father, you walked with the dead only for the purpose of burying them. You kept your hands out of the matter after that.

Glistening with sweat on this humid evening, my mother reminisced about the dog's fur, how it had a rough edge when you brushed her backside, how she licked water from the bowl starting from the outside rim, how she would jump at the maple trees when the leaves rustled. My mother drilled holes into some pennies with my father's tools and strung them together with yellow twine. A metal coat hanger held the dozen pennies just below the green awning, directly above our wicker chairs where Raisin had loved to curl up at night. My mother made as many wind chimes as she bought. Her handmade ones were always simple as the penny-chime, formed with items from around our house: cheap jewellery beads or mismatched cutlery, odd screws and long dangling earrings, pigeon feathers or pine combs from our lawn. But she handled them with as much care as she did store- or flea-market-bought ones of silver or blown glass, with brass or crystal weights, oil-painted tops, or intricately whittled wood. The homemade chimes were my favourites because my mother would preach to me as she made and hung them.

"Take this one here," she said, words slightly muffled by the twine she held in her mouth, one arm stretched out, the other struggling with scissors to snip it, chin jutting toward the sparkling stones excavated from an abandoned aquarium. One of her prettiest, the gold and silver flecks catching the light underneath the porch, it swayed easily in the wind, two gold Christmas reindeer bells tied underneath the lowest stones, an ocean-blue plastic Tupperware lid punctured with holes. "Your Uncle Danny once tried to rescue a little girl who fell through a melting lake near his house in Saskatchewan. Yes, there are lakes in Saskatchewan. Hills, too. He saw her arm rise above the water as he drove by. He jumped straight into the winter cold of that water. Unfortunately, she had already drowned." I'd heard the story before, but didn't mind. My mother had a story for each wind chime. She waved for me to take the scissors from her, and I did, imagining what it must have been like for Uncle Danny, who I had never met, to carry a dead girl out of those icy waters.

Most of the time I listened to my mother's sermons as if dreaming. I was intent on the words, but found them hard to gather inside my head. I'd start to itch, pressing the sides of my sneakers back and forth over the ground, enjoying the slight pain in my ankles the repetition caused. I know I've forgotten most of what she preached to me, but the hymns I'll never forget.

"Your mother's quite the singer," I remember our mailman calling out to me as he passed our property. He wasn't telling the truth, really. My mother didn't sing; she hummed. Her voice vibrated like an organ. When she sang I felt the same way I did when my father took me to his church on Sundays, kneeling on the hard wood as the music surrounded me. I was vaguely content, but only a listener of devotion. Later, I found out the nights she spent humming on our front porch with her collection of wind chimes bothered some of the neighbours. Not because of the noise, but because of the sight of her, rocking back and forth in her coat, staring out into the sky and praying, her collection of chimes rattling in her strong winds. The neighbours watched her the way one does a stray animal, and my mother would have been horrified if she'd known she was on display. "So stupid they are, not seeing what they should be seeing," I can imagine her saying, delicately pushing the dangling toes of one of her chimes to summon a domino effect down the whole stretch of the porch. Even my father was guilty some nights of watching her through the living-room window, perplexed and fascinated. She spoke a language he could never learn, although he never disrupted her mourning. But my sister, Katia, two years older than me, was averse to the porch because of it. She even went to school through the back door.

One wind chime for each of the dead, or so my mother claimed. Aunt Mary's chime had a cluster of sand dollars for a roof, with tiny, white, crystal moons and stars attached to brass cylinders, and it sounded like someone playing the spoons. My mother had bought it at a yard sale for a dollar fifty and stood beaming as I climbed one of the wicker chairs to help her hang it. "Oh, Mary, I just couldn't resist," she squealed as we turned the porch light on to admire it. An upbeat tune came out of my mother's lips like a whistle.

This time, my father had been trudging his way up to the house, his work boots drenched with mud from our yard left from a few nights of rain. His face had already begun to tighten and freeze over the last two years into lines and dry skin. Business was slow and he was worried. No one bought handcrafted chairs anymore, my mother said. He busied himself by building us trunks and dressers and a gazebo in the backyard, keeping his muscles working like an oiled machine. He almost walked straight past us until my mother's words registered. Then he swung around and held tightly to the stair banister, eyes already filling with tears.

"Mary's ... Mary's ... she's not ..."

"May as well be," my mother replied, reaching out to straighten the buckles on my father's overalls. "She hasn't visited us in five years."

"Jesus Christ, Maggie!" he screamed, and shook her by the shoulders, lifting her feet off the porch. Then, aware of what he was doing, he dropped her back down. I was embarrassed for him then. Aunt Mary was his sister, the youngest, married with one boy and another child on the way. He left us for the back-yard and we soon heard the familiar rhythms of the axe breaking firewood. My mother soothed her dishevelled dress, tucked her thin brown hair behind her ears, and sat leaning forward on her wicker chair, hands cupped under her chin. "I'm sorry," she said very quietly, like a child. And I loved her. Loved her for the wind chimes and her humming and her ways. A new line formed between my father's ordered firewood and my own place on the porch. I lay my head in my mother's lap and stayed there until my father couldn't take it anymore.

"I'll lock the door, Maggie, for the night, if you don't come in now." He said this to me, as if I were the one keeping her, or perhaps hurt I hadn't spent the evening with him. I had noticed him a few times through the window, sitting by the fire, picking up and discarding cards, books, and his smaller working tools, Katia, her back turned away from the window, adjusting chan-nels on the radio.

Mother nodded. "In a bit, please."

"Right now!"

The door slammed behind him, and the farthest wind chime, an imitation of a Prince Rupert's Drop, smashed against the railing. Shards of glass fell like hail.

Cover Before Striking

My father hardly ever yelled at her; this is one of the only times I can remember him doing so. They were loving parents. Not just to my sister and me, but to each other. Hugging in the backyard, my father's hands swimming over her dress and my mother shoving him playfully away only to grab his head, sometimes slick with sweat, into her hands so she could plant kisses over his lips and bushy eyebrows. So close that his wrinkles, which were now crow's feet, seemed to belong to her.

When my mother lay dying in the city hospital, I felt she'd been cheated, that the music she'd created for the dead abandoned her at her own. The cancer had spread into her throat, making it difficult to understand anything she said. She hated the indoors, had spent little time or money decorating the rooms of our house; my parents' bedroom housed a double bed, a night table with three framed pictures: their wedding and one of Katia and one of me, and a simple pine dresser and a rocking chair, all crafted by my father. She preferred to be outdoors, seasons changing around her, smells of fields and wildflowers. Now she had a window with the view of the connecting wings. Eyes limp, hair reduced to fine layers of black and white, lips loose, she blended into the white nightgown the hospital made her wear. The only noise came from the machine bleating monotonously about her confused face. My father would stare out the window, his hand against the glass like a flag, as my mother struggled to mouth simple words. *Water. Washroom. Love.* Or was it *Live*?

My mother owned at least eight dozen wind chimes in the end, most kept in boxes in the hallway closet near the front door. Many were for friends or relatives, and many for animals, too, mostly stray cats we had taken to feeding. Sometimes she also hung them for people she had never met; children on the news; who'd died in accidents were transformed into trinkets or beads, bound by twine or string. When the Mayfield Public School bus crashed five miles from our home and two teenagers died, she told me the chimes would help deliver their souls to safety. To her, every soul was worth saving. As in church, salvation came from believing in forces one couldn't see, such as the wind. I remember chimes as plain as standard playing cards or rusted nails, others resembling circus carousels, brightly varnished birds or angels, glittering cylinders and lace-covered bells. The only criterion was music, whether a curt ting or a euphonic melody.

"My childhood sweetheart died trying to fly," I remember her telling me once as we watched the chimes swaying gently, nearly imperceptibly, on a summer night. For years, I imagined him like me, with short brown hair and square knee caps, diving from the top of a hayloft and crashing through the floorboards, skull split open and legs twisted, a protruding form underneath the wreck. But I had it all wrong. He'd died in a sledding accident. Snapped his neck. Instantly. Without pain. When I found out the truth, I imagined him trapped in the cold snow, slush down his throat, waiting for my mother to dig him out.

She didn't always wait for the anniversary of his death to bring out his wind chime. My father wasn't a jealous man and her deep attachment to the boy never stirred him. "He was older than your mom," he told me. "He kept the other kids from teasing her. She had a lisp then, and the kids made fun of how she talked." It startled me to learn that my mother had faults, especially faults in her speech, since she always corrected me if I mumbled or dropped my g's. "He helped her, and I suppose she loved him as much as any twelve year-old could." Although

I wasn't twelve yet, I could picture my mother kissing this boy's lips and running her hands all over his face. Open-mouthed, his hands on her waist. I saw him pushing his way tenderly underneath her skirt, humming into her ear. I knew it was this boy who had taught her to sing.

She brought out his chime on foggy nights, air so thick it pushed to the back of my throat when I breathed. His was pewter, and weighed more than any other. A carousel of wings. My mother would shake in her chair, humming, keeping warm by breathing her song into wool mittens. My father forbade me to stay outside with her those nights in case I caught cold. I'd sulk in the warmth of the living room, Katia teasing me that I was acting like a girl.

"It's easier to fly if you can't see the ground," she instructed, rocking methodically before my father demanded that I remain inside.

I nodded, though I did not understand. The strings rubbed together like vibrating cymbals. The boy with twisted legs appeared in the shadowy snow before me, bones piled like firewood.

"Dust does not return to dust. The only thing that keeps him here is the weight."

I couldn't bear to bring her flowers in the hospital, though I imagine the presence of them would have pleased her. I felt as if I'd be burying her in the room right then and there if I did; a signal we were out of hope. For weeks before she died I dreamed of building her coffin myself from the planks off our old porch, though if one of us had been capable of doing so, it would have been my father. In the dreams my desire was strong, but I still lacked the skill. The coffin, its boards slanted and unsymmetrical, resembled all the awkward ashtrays and picture frames I made to please her as a child.

Even though I call it mourning, my mother was rarely depressed on her porch surrounded by the dead. They kept her company. Or maybe she kept them company. Dates didn't mean much to her. "A night like this" was enough to call it an anniversary, whether three times a year or once in five. Weather played an essential role. Generally, animals were mourned in the spring as mothers gave birth to new litters. Grandma Barnes was mourned with the first berries in our garden and a child who died when her body rejected a new heart with a crackle of sheet lightning. "There you are," she would exclaim as she produced the correct chime, turning her flushed face to me. "Remember me?"

Yet a couple of years after the incident with Aunt Mary's wind chime, I no longer felt the desire to join her out on the porch. Perhaps it's my imagination, but she didn't seem to mind. It coincided with my refusal to go to Sunday church. My father went to church more out of habit than any religious conviction, and I, turning eleven that year, wasn't interested in being anyone's disciple, at home or outside. I was getting older, more cynical, beginning to see my mother through the eyes of a critical neighbour, one who might tell a child, "Your mother's quite the singer." Since my father and sister never joined her congregation of death, my shame was lessened. I thought, like Judas, I could still kiss and betray my mother at the same time. I did betray her though, in my heart. I was embarrassed by her open displays of the dead, the constant buzz and whine and twang of the porch. I desired silence.

I absolved myself of any connection to her nightly chorus. When teenagers stopped to stare or laugh at her, or when teased at school, I'd pretend I had no idea what my mother was doing outside humming with a collection of wind chimes. I even did cruel imitations of her so my schoolmates would know I realized how silly she was. I thought of her as possessed or diseased. I rarely invited anyone to the house. But our backyard was large, clear of trees except as a border, and on one occasion I did, to practise with the captain of the softball team. My mother had kept vigil on the porch every evening that week because someone had stolen one of her chimes. She'd bought it for a Native teenager who was beaten to death by a police officer in Toronto. She'd found the painted mask and fake arrowheads at a craft sale. After checking each of her boxes over and over, she resorted to asking neighbours, none of whom took her distress seriously. I could hear her in the front while we played, moaning like an injured animal.

"Hey," the Christie kid said, sticking his tongue out to one side, "your mother is crazy."

"At least she's sober," I retorted. We could all hurt each other through the acts of our parents, and I knew the Christies were known for drinking. Patrol cars frequently took his father home as he yelled that he had every damn right to drink as much as he liked, he lived in a democracy, didn't he? This time I couldn't stand it, my mother wailing like a cat in heat, the clutter of the chimes over the archway of the house. The Christie kid wouldn't stop teasing me, only pausing when my father came outside to saw wood into planks.

"Gotta use the bathroom," I said, and headed to the front. My mother was gazing down the road, perhaps waiting for her dead to stroll in for a cup of tea or lay their heads on her lap where mine used to rest.

"Be quiet," I hissed.

She stepped back and stumbled, hitting a copper chime with the back of her head, the buzz echoing in my ears. I approached her again.

"Just shut up! The dead can't hear you!"

I was shocked by my own words. My mother took another step back. Then she turned away, her back shaking. I was glad. I had no desire to touch her. I went to the backyard and told the Christie kid to go home.

"Going to sing with your mommy?" he taunted, my father in the far corner working on the gazebo.

I struck him as hard as I could in the stomach. He doubled over, dropping the baseball bat. I picked it up. Bathed in a cold sweat, my tears couldn't be detected, or if they could it was obvious the Christie kid was still afraid.

"Take it back!" I demanded, threatening to strike. "Take it back!"

He nodded vigourosly. "Okay. Okay. I take it back," he relented, scrambling to get up, holding his stomach with his hands.

I dropped the bat. The Christie kid gathered his breath. Before tearing down the path of the driveway, he shoved his hands into his pocket and threw what I thought were tiny stones at me. I went back to the front to find my mother slouched against her chair, pounding her fists against her knees. Without a word, I threw the arrowheads the Christie kid had flung at me into her lap. I was worse than the Judas I'd imagined. I was Peter, denying her over and over.

After the funeral, my father put all of my mother's wind chimes into cardboard boxes, and stored them in the gazebo. He couldn't throw them out, the way other widowers can't bear to give away their spouse's clothes. "But I can't have them in the house," he said, taping the lids shut like cheap coffins. "I just ... I can't."

Eventually I took them off his hands. Cynthia and I brought

them with us to our new bungalow in Toronto. I remembered how for years while my mother was alive a silent fear hung over my childhood home that perchance coming up the walkway after school a new wind chime might mysteriously appear belonging to my father, Katia, or me, the way one appeared one after-rain day for Aunt Mary. We never thought of one for my mother. She was the keeper of souls, not a soul herself.

After my betrayal, I feared I would be included with Aunt Mary in her mourning, that when my mother saw some boys playing catch she might sing for the day I made her cry on our porch. She didn't, though, and later when I longed for the sounds of her humming and the ominous beauty of her chimes, she let me back into her congregation. As unquestioningly as she hung a chime for a newborn found in the town dump, she welcomed me again to her family of the dead.

Without her guidance, I had no idea what to do with the boxes. I dreamed about them and her, and spoke of them so often that I believe it's what spurred Cynthia to fix those that were broken or time-beaten. Wind chimes are very fragile, especially homemade ones, and Cynthia has discovered she has a skill for the craft. Something to keep her busy while she was pregnant, she said. She painted and polished, sanded and dusted, until the basement was as littered with song as the old porch, except for the lack of a singer.

My father and Katia dealt with my mother's death the same way they dealt with all death. They walked in silence. Katia, her fine features physically closest to our mother's, visited the cemetery on the first anniversary and surrounded her grey marble stone with bright spring flowers. My mother had died while rain, the heavy kind that makes it difficult to breathe, fell persistently.

The patter on the window took over the monotony from the turned-off machines. And since we later buried her under a stark sun, it is hard not to be reminded of my mother's death in almost any weather except snowfall. She is too light for snowfall.

Today my daughter was baptized, and Father and Katia returned to our house, Father dressed in a new brown suit, his shoulders turned in with age, brimming with pride at his granddaughter. Katia appeared old as well, older than her age, as silent as my father. For the afternoon it seemed as if Mother were with him, her arm around his waist, blessing the new life entering our family. Over the last eight months I'd searched my daughter's face for traces of my mother, a changing eye colour or a narrow, slanted nose, but she resembled my wife's side of the family. I was constantly disappointed. But this evening we took everyone into the baby's room to lay our daughter inside her crib. The wind chimes Cynthia restored glowed like stars or halos suspended from the ceiling with the light from the window. As the initial shock of my mother's presence subsided, my father took Katia's hand into his own. The fingers of his other hand gently squeezed the air, and I suspect he held on to something unseen but worth remembering. We waited for the baby to sleep. My child, captured by the dance of legs rubbing in the wind, opens her mouth. She cannot speak; she hums. And now there are two tunes.

Sleepwalking

At first we were as honoured as the other parts of her body: her delicate hands, the square fingers that pushed against objects as if trying to hold them by sheer will; her eyes, blue at birth and then a dull grey, slightly small, almost oriental; her thick hair, even then the shade of oak bark. We were tickled and dusted with talcum powder. We were slipped into fresh cotton socks and tiny white sneakers. People crowded us, comparing the size of their own to ours. Olivia, or as her parents called her, Ollie, was in perfect proportion, until she no longer had anyone to depend on to look out for us. Until she learned how to walk. Then, because she assumed our movements were unconscious, she forgot who was responsible for keeping her up. Ollie the baby was perfect, a sylvan shepherdess; Ollie the adolescent wondered about her hands.

Thin white polyester gloves with sheer frills and tiny yellow flowers. Long purple silk gloves with pointed ends. Pink woollen gloves with bobbles of faux fur. Tiny red buttons, miniature hearts, on cream lace. And a dozen mittens. Ollie's parents spoiled her hands, let her sleep with gloves on, saying her "Lord's Prayer" and "Hail Mary" and "If I Die Before I Wake." She seemed a quiet nun at peace with her vanity. The parents approved, the neighbours approved, and the teachers thought her "precious." No one condescended to see how we were doing. Not even the doctors who pricked her fingertips (after asking her three time to remove her lovely gloves) seemed to think our blood needed tending. We became grave, and if truth be told, as it must, we became jealous. Weren't we, after all, the prime movers of her universe? That's what we thought.

We decided to sleep all day. Ollie tripped, bumped, slid, fell, toppled, teetered, trampled. Ollie could not tap dance or play basketball. Ollie could not climb ladders or jump rope. We were delighted. As an unseen consequence, however, Ollie relied further on her hands. They slammed against floors and cupboards to support her, protect her face. They waltzed around the young boys' bodies seductively, so that they didn't care whether she could be dipped or twirled. They moved in front of her, tentatively, instinctively, like the blind. They developed their own language. And we were sore. We wanted to run. We too wanted to feel. We wanted Ollie to watch where she was going.

It came to us as a just revenge. Wriggling and anxious after having slept all day, we needed to stretch. Like a hypnotist we summoned inner strength, staunch desire, made all her matter bend to our will. We slipped off the bed, and, a little frightened by the possibility of her entire body at our command, we simply stood in the dark, pressing our heels into the carpet, unbelieving. We went back to bed, blood racing, causing our limbs to twitch. Then we crashed on our own titillation. That was the first night.

The second night (we waited three days for the second night — how we did this we still don't know, perhaps afraid we would lose the gift) we became bolder. Found out her hands could be instructed to place a towel underneath her blankets and turn a doorknob. We were on our way outside before her mother, Mommy (still at fifteen), called Ollie. We stopped in our tracks and waited to see if Ollie would wake. She didn't. We kept on through the kitchen as Mommy ran down the stairs and turned on lights. The mysterious night, which we ached to examine and which had left its corners exposed like unravelled bandages a moment ago, had now sealed itself back up. We were cheated, we thought, until Mommy put a hand on her daughter, and gently directed her upstairs. Apparently, Mommy had previously witnessed this phenomenon. Olivia was regarded as normal. Unconsciousness, like puberty, though disorienting, was a natural state. We stayed and pondered the consequences for a long time.

Initially, the park was our first goal. The vibrant green blades of grass our imagined bed. We trained. Used our momentum to get a little farther each night. To the kitchen, to the door, the end of the gravel driveway, the dull wattage lampposts behind the large maple in front. At times Mommy came and retired us, and once Father overheard us and started to call for Ollie, but Mommy stopped him. Something about "never wake up the sleepwalking, they don't know where they are and panic." Olivia never knew where she was. Inwardly we chuckled. Proper attire was analyzed. She had only three pairs of shoes, a sadly deficient ratio to her litanies of gloves. Blue tartan slippers that turned our skin red, the soles worn and made for slipping, the colour cracked like leftover hardened dough. Ash-grey sneakers that hardly sneaked, but creaked incessantly with every push against the floor, yet at least they were comfortable, well-fitted, a perfectly snug size five and a half. And a black dress shoe, a shiny plastic made to resemble leather, with a warbled rose on each ankle, a slight square heel. We wore those in churches and decorated houses in winter. Not very often. Olivia repeatedly fell. She could not balance us, though we tried to form to her gravity, her equilibrium, gain inertia. The dynamics were wrong. We were worn out and bruised by these three. Cages instead of cloaks. We would have to be the eyes, make sure nothing was in Olivia's way. Our decision: bare was the way to go.

When we broke the street barrier and wandered upon the cold concrete sidewalk the night was unusually humid, and the cold perspiration caused Ollie twice to sneeze. We stopped and tried to decipher whether her eyes were still closed. Sometimes it was hard to tell the difference with Ollie. With Olivia, too. We leapt over the chain that announced the entry into the park and the new taste of the generously watered grass was glorious. For once, we, who moved in synchronicity instinctively with the other, were broken apart by the touch of the ground. We demanded that Ollie sit down with her knees pointed in opposite directions and we stared at each other. The black and grey patches of dirt, the white calluses and flaked red slivers of dead skin transformed into honourable scars and bruises. The mirror of our sole was one of resistance.

"Cm'ear, cm'ear." We jumped back into our unity, startled by the murmuring voice. Olivia hadn't budged an inch, though we hadn't yet asked her to, either. "Cm'ear, grrrrl." The man looked around the same age as Father, but smelled older, reeked of stacked sweat. "Grrrl." The air grew thicker, the grass began to suffocate us, and yet we stayed, unwilling to give up. The man wore boots, a deep tan brown with torn black laces that dragged along the ground with the tongues clipped. His voice had grown more distinct in his approach and we could see the black curly hair on his knees poke through the rips in his jeans. He dropped his pants. Olivia said nothing. She saw nothing. She heard nothing. We did. It was the first time we saw that part of a man. We felt a certain sympathy for it. It seemed as neglected as we were.

In the morning Olivia didn't bother to check her feet. If she had, she would have pondered the dirt in our nails, and the glow that radiated regardless. That day we couldn't sleep. We bounced Ollie to school, and although she felt a little sore, she blamed it on her young body, governed by conspiracy, a body she figured had its own mind with its erratic spurts and cycles, its moodiness and deceit. Curiously, when she touched her body with her gloves on, there was harmony. Ollie spoke beautifully with her hands. We must give her that. That night, and on two other occasions that week, we went back to the park. Then we walked around the block, down to the corner store that merged with the long crescent adjacent to the park, and up the hill where the older houses hovered. Sometimes we saw people, and sometimes we floated like shadows. She wrapped her arms around her knees when she was sore. Mommy gave her Aspirin. Ollie sensed she was blooming and became excitable, demanded a new dress and a set of crushed-velvet gloves. Both the same colour as her blood, but she didn't tell Mommy that.

We discovered quickly that we could only push ourselves so far. We were still limited by skeletons, by natural obstacles. We could not hold Ollie up twenty-four hours a day, as much as we desired it. We became bloated and sore. We chafed and peeled. We enlarged and needed rest. Limiting ourselves to once a week, our exploits had to make themselves count. We wanted to try on different shapes for size: mud, rain water, and weeds, to name a few. We grew bolder, even though during the days we had no idea what new appendage we would awake to find: a scratch, splinter, a new and aching tumour. Olivia was torturing us, and we, like sado-masochists, took every blow in stride.

On the eve of a party, we were treated to silk lining as she shoved us, cramped and swollen, into new black heels and danced on a gymnasium floor. The brief intercourse with her hands, adorned with the blood-red velvet gloves, had left us unsatisfied. We wanted her to grace us with her soft caress, but once again, it was saved for others. A young man, tall and slim, confident in beige leather loafers, held us up. We tried to stay in tune with him, from gym to cab to wooden stairs. Olivia did not understand what was expected of her. She tossed off our coffins and we melted onto wool. Alone with the lights turned off and murmuring voices on either side. Young noise. No adults. We pressed lightly against the back of his leg as he tried to unbutton her dress. "This is nice," he said over and over as if reciting a hymn.

"Ummm," Olivia answered.

But when her dress was unbuttoned and fell on top of us, she withdrew sharply and said, "I want to sleep now." If we hadn't felt so estranged from Ollie, maybe we wouldn't have. But maybe we would. It's difficult to say. But certainly we would have waited until she asked us to act for her. Friction was our only defense against numbness. We wrapped ourselves around his torso, skin on unfamiliar skin exciting us deliciously. He fell on her like snow. In the morning, Ollie put on her bra, and the young man worshipped her, his eyes sparkling at her every gesture. "Do that again, what you did last night."

She laughed.

"Come on, don't get shy with me. Do that thing you did … you know … with your … your …"

Olivia kissed him passionately and giggled. The young man's anticipatory limb deflated in disappointment.

"You have no direction," Mommy said once the short walks to school and back were over. "What are you going to do?" Olivia kicked us against the legs of her chair, the fluff on her slippers between us. The act of wearing new high heels the night before had consequences. We had bruises matching the curve in our toes. We were also tired and weary, the night's abuse upon our skin, a new and strange sensation so unlike her usual clumsiness, a sleepiness and a determination all at the same time that came over us the course of the whole night. Awake yet not awake. We had not been able at times to sense the floor. Getting worse over the night, turning in and out at the wrong moments, without enough water to sustain movement, although Olivia was always sipping a glass. Our senses disoriented, in a haze. *Has she been sleepwalking without us?* we wondered.

"You have no direction," Mommy continued, the world spinning in nausea. "What are you going to do?"

Ollie … Ollie … Your bones are broken. Olivia, one man is dead. Ollie, if you can, you must awaken. Or at least speak. Your bones are broken and the floor is wet. The house is asleep except for us. The air is getting harder to gather and your hands have stopped moving.

Olivia married a man wearing short, dark-blue leather boots with a reinforced heel. That night we stayed awake, as did Ollie, and felt her blood rise and fall in the man's hands. The man known to the world as Joshua. He laid her out on the bed and we faced him as he bent down and kissed us. We had encountered him before, but not like this, and not usually with Ollie awake. Invigorated, we thought this might be the end, no need to wake at night for attention. He kissed, his warm hot mouth upon us, each for each. He rubbed us up, and Ollie rippled. *Love* was the word he used. "This is love," we repeated, over and over, that warm protected feeling of letting ourselves be raised up in someone's hands.

Two years we were in love. His feet beautifully crafted, like candle-holders, with reddish-brown hair sprouting on his toes and up his shins. We snuggled against them and they smelled like grass. We walked in time on the street. Olivia joked that she must have finally adjusted to her bones because she hadn't tripped in so long. We slept and woke according to their internal clocks. We sometimes wrapped around them like wings, thinking we could fly, forgetting the ground. Joshua had even mentioned once when the lights were on, "Ol, I think your feet are tired. You should give them a good soak in the bath." We were in heaven. Ollie's dexterous hands smoothed and soothed the years over. We forgave her everything. Ollie, we did, you know, no matter what happened after. We forgave you, even if you are still responsible.

We spent a lot of time in the attic, especially when there was less "work" for Ollie. The bright lights snapping over her hands on a table. Hand Model, they called her, diligently fussing over her already spoiled fingers and wrists, the sheer amount of attention on them enough to make them glow. But we didn't mind anymore. The attic was our time. Renovated into a sewing room for Ollie and her gloves. Protectors of her livelihood. We pushed against pedals all day, the rhythm contagious. Silk, satin, cotton, sheer, Lycra swept over us in droves, Ollie finishing one and letting it drop on top of us to start straight on the other. The hum of the machine accentuated our push. We made beautiful music together, the three of us. Daily life took on a melody. Except Joshua wasn't there, and seemed to be there less, as if we were ghosts and haunted him only in the middle of the night, our chains rattling precisely.

Ollie had been drinking the night everything changed. She didn't know, but we could smell her. Patterns we came to recognize. We would feel safe, relaxed, and then desire seized us rapturously and we needed to move, push, swell, taunt, flirt, until we stumbled and ached, until we were too full of ourselves and then were empty. We were in the mood for Joshua. We came from a party, a party without Joshua, who needed to "catch up." We had it planned, Ollie included, to drape ourselves on top of him the second we got through the bedroom door. The stairs echoed our intent, thirteen of them, just enough time as a warning. Ollie opened the door in her light, turquoise, satin elbow-length dress gloves like a sleight-of-hand expert. Joshua was in bed. Ollie giggled, "I see you were thinking of me."

"I see you've been drinking," he replied. "I can smell you from here."

Ollie leaned against the mattress to give him a kiss. He accepted, rustling her hair. But we could see Her, underneath the bed, completely naked, her feet poking out and waving at us mockingly. She was holding her breath.

Ollie began to sleepwalk again. Joshua learned to live with it, barely got up after a couple of months to check where she was going. Knowing he might be suspicious, we were careful. We took her to the attic, or to the kitchen. Eventually out to the garden. He got used to the sound of the door opening and closing. He didn't worry. Everything was fine. Ollie, of course, still did not know about the woman underneath the bed. Her head was in the clouds. We were down in the dirt and kept the secret weighed within us like the heart of a well. Not that we still didn't rise to Joshua in the night. Frequently we forced Ollie to roll on top of him, pound him into her as if she could nail him there, force the truth out of him. The heights we reached were exhilarating, all of us passing out like balloons drained of air. Joshua looked forward to those nights. So did we.

Joshua, Joshua, Joshua. Your name a mantra we repeated with every stroke upon the ground in the darkness. Joshua, Joshua, we went back to the park, a new park, and found some lonely men. Joshua, Joshua, we brought your Ollie to all-night coffee shops and train stations. Joshua, Joshua, her eyes were open while she slept. Joshua, we could've killed you at any time.

One autumn night late in October, while the tired leaves fell, the stale smell of fire, we rose red as flames, musky. Down the street was a man whom Joshua knew and later knew Ollie. They saw each other about once a month and earlier that evening they had been at his place having a couple of drinks. This man was a "bachelor." Joshua joked that he liked "the good life." His floor had obviously not been cleaned in a while but was decent, with only a slight film of dust and debris. He wore casuals up to his neck. Ollie had left her purse and meant to retrieve it in the morning. This man was the one we wanted while the world changed colour, while the winds breezed by the moon. Ollie provided the means.

With Patrick, things got very complicated. Ollie did not respond to him if he stopped by during the day to see her on his lunch hour or if he dropped by to ask them out for dinner. At night he taunted her for her afternoon modesty. Ripping off her clothes, spreading us apart savagely, he told her she was "the perfect woman." We knew this was not love, but it was addicting, absorbing all our energy to keep up with him. Not just rooms with beds, but all rooms, all surfaces we felt: rugs, wood, hard glass, upholstery. A couple of nights he reversed, his hands holding us, grabbing us as his head bent into her wet thighs. We saw the floor from a whole new angle. Tried to mimic his inventiveness. His feet lithe like a dancer's. We brought him to orgasm once through his pants, massaging him. If only Olivia had known we could perform as well as her delicate hands. At times she would wake confused, half-believing her dreams. "It was so real, Joshua, my dream last night."

"It's like you have another life when you're asleep," he told her, amazed by the parts she felt able to tell him, how she could feel wind, actually feel it on her hair and legs in a dream.

"Are you sure, honey, are you sure I've never left the house?"

Joshua was sure. "You always come to me." He did not suspect the detours before arriving.

Patrick kissed Ollie while awake. Ollie was stunned, but kissed back. Ollie then said she didn't think it was a good idea to see him anymore. Patrick laughed. Ollie asked him to leave. Patrick protested and tried to kiss her again. Ollie turned her face and he caught her neck. She lingered there. Joshua was out. Patrick had dropped by. Olivia was lonely, so lonely. She didn't know Patrick was worshipping her at night. She had not felt Joshua through her hands in months. Patrick kissed her neck. "I've never cheated on Joshua," she whispered, breathing heavily. "You're supposed to be his friend." Patrick hesitated. "And you're supposed to be his wife," he said. Winter was coming.

Ollie went to see Patrick. "I've dreamed about you for weeks now," she admitted.

"When do you sleep?"

"I dream in my sleep about you." Patrick played the new game, bringing her a drink, lighting a candle, holding her model hands. "There are times I feel like I don't know what I'm doing."

He gently took off her blouse, then her bra, then her skirt, and then her stockings, admiring every piece like on her wedding night with Joshua. "Neither do I." But oh, how he did. We didn't return to Joshua until morning. Luckily, he was still asleep. He turned to Ollie, but Ollie refused, faking dreams by closing her eyes.

Ollie, your hands are bleeding. Can't you feel them, Ollie? Can't you pay attention to us now, Ollie? We need you. Your hands are bleeding and your ribs are broken. You must trust us. You must believe us. Ollie, the man beside you is dead and we need to get out of here. Ollie, the house is asleep. Asleep. It is up to you.

The rest happened quickly. Patrick knew Olivia during the day and Ollie at night. Joshua knew nothing. The other woman too had stopped coming; everything she kept at the house was kept under the bed, and one day the floor was clean. We could see straight through to the bathroom. Joshua doted on Ollie. Ollie turned away. Only once in a while, when we woke and felt sorry for what we'd done, did we go back to him. He moved like a stranger in the park. Ollie drank a little more than usual. Patrick did, too. We were all sore. The nights full of anxiety and the days full of plotting. We had insomnia. Things got very mixed up, very mixed up indeed.

To the bank machine three blocks away we sent her, and she withdrew money from the accounts. That was Monday. On Tuesday we sent her to the travel agency to pick up tickets. On Wednesday Joshua pushed her and started crying, asking her why she didn't love him anymore. On Wednesday Ollie made love to him and he clung to her chest all night. On Thursday she went to see Patrick and he came in her mouth three times. On Friday she prepared a big dinner for both of them. It was planned the month before. On Saturday she packed a few toiletries and all her precious gloves. On Sunday she planned to leave.

Joshua was supposed be out of town until Monday for a convention. Patrick was in the house, in their bed. Patrick loved being in the house, he told her. "It's like pretending I'm not a bachelor," he said. But she was still asleep. We had invited him in the middle of the night. Ollie had only meant to fake a trip to her parents and escape for a week in Mexico with Patrick. We planned not to let her return. Joshua came home early. We heard him, but it felt like a dream, and turning over we kicked Patrick. He heard the door. Ollie fell back asleep and so did we. We awoke to noise below. The body beside us felt like Patrick's and we let him sleep, took the steps carefully to the first floor in our grogginess. As we approached the basement, we realized all our plans might be foiled, and the plane was leaving in less than three hours. We panicked.

The front door was open and violent gusts of snow were flung into the open doorway. The basement stairs creaked and we took Ollie there, determined not to be caught with Patrick upstairs. Determined to get away. We placed Ollie by the door, shivering, and as the door pushed onto us, we banged it shut. Nothing. Opened it. That's when we heard the scream and the banister break. Ollie had woken, disoriented, and we lost our balance in shock. We tripped down the stairs, and without a banister to grab for, Ollie's hands cracked against the concrete. Beside her, a man. Both unconscious.

Cover Before Striking

We noticed the blood right away. Skull split. Face against the floor. Joshua, Joshua, Joshua. We hadn't meant for it to turn out this way. We hadn't meant for things to go this far. Ollie shouldn't have woken. It was unnatural. Unnatural. Joshua. Your head is cracked and only now that the light is on can we make any attempt at a last look at love. Your face is hidden, but your feet, in the light, the bright light in front of us, are dizzying. Blinding. Ollie cannot see you, though her eyes are open. Joshua, Joshua, why did you come home? Ollie's bones are broken and your breath has stopped. Joshua, you never had such shoes before. Joshua, you are wearing Patrick's shoes. Patrick, wake up. Come and deliver us. The door is open and the snow is piling.

> Ollie, pay attention. Joshua is sleeping and you
> have broken bones.
> Your hands are crushed into stars and we are
> fading.
> Olivia, we are about to fall asleep.
> Olivia we trust
> that when we do you will awake.
> Olivia.

Three Days Left

The stewardess was middle-aged, but dressed in a short skirt and low-cut blazer she looked younger, reddish-brown wavy hair held up by two matching blue barrettes. She smiled and offered David his complimentary pillow and blanket, her bust angled generously for a quick view. As she tilted her head to attend to the next aisle, David caught her gently by the arm. He looked out the window next to the emergency door at the deep blue sky and white pompous clouds. "I'm sorry. I must be very tired," he told her.

She adjusted her hair, tucking a loose strand behind her ears. "Yes?"

"I can't seem to remember where this plane is going."

"Going?"

"Yes, I'm sorry ... I'm not feeling well."

She gestured toward his sickness bag.

"No, I just need to know where we're going. I mean, am I on my way to Florida? My mother lives in Florida."

"No," she replied, "but we might be on the way to see your father."

"My father. My father is ..."

"We stay in the sky. Don't you remember? A new kind of vacation for a new kind of life?" She dropped a glossy pamphlet in his lap on top of the complimentary blanket, smiled dutifully, and continued down the aisle.

Why spend thousands of dollars on hotels and restaurants on your vacation? said a beautiful woman in a pink business suit to an equally good-looking though dishevelled girlfriend. *Why? When nine times out of ten it rains and your wallet gets stolen?* He turned the page and both women were now dressed in light cotton sundresses, lounging in airplane chairs with tall colourful drinks in their hands, sharing a good joke. *Why bother? When you can get carried into the air and served like a queen without leaving your chair or your country?* The girls laughed and drank and laughed and drank and David looked around him and he was the only one alone. There were young men chatting with young women and couples playing cards and food being ordered from shiny menus and many a person with headphones watching movies and eating popcorn when all of a sudden David's emergency window opened.

He awoke to find himself choking on grass, spitting green back onto the earth. He had no idea how long he had been unconscious, but Old Magnum was back in his usual spot against his fence, and David was close to his. The awning had not been rewound and he was glad for the shade. He knelt in front of the fence and locked himself back in. David was only mildly uncomfortable. The handcuff could slide up and down half a foot from the ground, dangling like a large bracelet. The new rhododendrons Julia had just planted were in his sight, and the smell of Old Magnum, the beagle next door, on the other side of the fence reminded him of long summer evenings he'd spent as a kid running with friends and their dogs in the rain. He breathed deeply and tried to regain his composure. He was a man on vacation, technically speaking. He had three days left of a nine-day hiatus from the advertising agency and a list of things he'd wanted to complete at home. Julia couldn't get time off work from the hospital, so they'd agreed to take a real vacation, technically speaking, after Christmas. He thought of the email he had received from his mother two weeks earlier. *I think I'm going to move in with Gloria. We've lost a lot of years, her and I. I'm starting to feel young again, like when we were kids and would share our secrets. I've never been happier, David, though I miss your father. But he's not really the man I knew, you understand. I can't go back. I'm resting.* He had not been surprised at her decision, though he had thought it would be a couple of years yet before she would move away. Or that maybe she would wait until his father actually died. *If you don't mind, I would like you to sell the house. Unless, of course, you want it.* He didn't know what he wanted. He had planned on building three new bookshelves, fixing the garage door problem, and assembling a hockey net replete with shooting targets. These plans were pinned with a magnet to the refrigerator. He had completed one black-painted pine bookshelf and the hockey net was in pieces in the garage with the garage door problem. His right hand, the one in the handcuff chained to the fence, had two calluses from use of the Allen key. He hadn't wanted to end up in the backyard again. The job shouldn't have been stressful. The box had set him off. It had claimed: *Learn to shoot like the professionals. Improved skills guaranteed. Be a Champion.* David had thrown the box to the side of the garage, maybe the side with the problem. The next thing David knew, he had chained himself to the fence. If he didn't want to keep his childhood home, he wanted to do a good job selling it.

David scanned his backyard. They owned a light-green wooden patio, four white plastic lounge chairs, a shovel, an electric barbecue, a small garden, a fence, and steel handcuffs. He couldn't imagine moving, but they couldn't afford to keep this house and his parents' house. They'd had both kids while living here. He'd been promoted here. Julia had thrown her baby showers here. They renovated the kitchen only last year to make room for a larger table and a dishwasher. He'd loved Julia here many times, a couple of times outside with the awning out when they had felt adventurous. He'd stroked her hair in the sun here, felt her legs, kissed her arms which she now held when sleeveless, trying to hide her soft biceps. He'd watched Gregory catch his first baseball in his first baseball mitt here. Ellen had landed her first cartwheel not a foot away from where he sat, yelling, "Daddy! Daddy!"

David shifted his weight off his elbow and with his free hand hiked up the waist of his pants in a sideways shuffle. He was hungry now. Famished. His stomach cramped. He unlocked the cuffs and stretched, unwinding as if he'd been immersed in water for hours. His limbs even felt shrivelled. It was easier to do than earlier, when Julia was home, standing on the patio, the red heart-shaped key dangling from her hand, coaxing him to take off the handcuffs and come back inside. "Okay, David," she'd said. "Why don't I make some tea or get you a glass of wine or something. Would you like that?" But he wouldn't budge. She couldn't convince him, and he could see her, for an hour, watching him from the kitchen window behind sheer white curtains. She'd left for work without speaking a further word to him. Now he strode toward the back door as if floating, his steps exaggerated, his body lithe. For a brief moment he had the urge to dance, but he didn't want to be seen. He opened the door and hopped inside. The percolator was on, heating stale coffee. A glass of white wine sounded wonderful. He cut an apple on the counter into sections, then ate, relishing every bite, the bruised sections mushy against his teeth. He opened the fridge. Maybe he would feel better if he made himself a huge meal, a gourmet feast, some veal cutlets and Caesar salad and scalloped potatoes with thick cheese and cream. He foraged around. All he had was half a dozen eggs, some blue cheese, and leftover pasta in tomato sauce. The wine bottle in the fridge was almost empty and about a week old. He sat down, picked up the phone, heard the dial tone, and set it down again. He went back outside, saluting Old Magnum who had fallen asleep and was snoring, and chained himself to the fence.

He tried to cloud-gaze and found not a single interesting shape to grab his imagination. He tried to remember the last time he felt happy. He wished Julia were home, even if she was angry. He wanted her to rip the cuffs off and tell him what to do, what to eat, where to go, how to spend the last days of his vacation, technically speaking. He counted blades of grass and grew dizzy. He broke open a dandelion and tasted the sour milk. He spread himself over the grass, his belly to the ground, and began to shiver. He pissed in the open air. The sun was losing its hold on the day. A mosquito bit his neck. David recalled the cool mist that had come over the Boy Scout camp that summer when he was ten. His mother was constantly sending him packages: cookies, gummy candies, mosquito repellent, extra socks, and cards that she had obviously signed on behalf of his father. On the day the Jenkins' kid, Stevie, had drowned, David had been eating his mother's chocolate chip cookies and reading her letter alone in his cabin. A few of the boys in the older division had taken out one of the canoes without permission, gone past the buoys without life jackets, and raced back to shore. Stevie never finished. The older boys and counsellors searched the water. David continued to eat his mother's chocolate chip cookies. They were all bused home the next day and his mother bought him his first real suit to attend Stevie's funeral. It was the last time he was sent to Boy Scout camp, or any other camp for that matter. He had never since felt so calm.

Julia came back with a movie and held it in front of him. He had taken off the handcuffs when he heard the car backing into the driveway, and hoped he looked presentable. He cursed himself for not having thought ahead and changing his dirty shirt. She waved the DVD as if it were a treat. "Thought you might be up for a comedy. We can watch it with the kids when they finish their homework."

"Okay," David agreed, though he didn't think he was in the mood for a comedy. But Julia had nothing to do with the hand-cuffs. She had begged him to relax on his vacation, to do only what he wanted to do.

"So …" she started, that settled. "What did you do today?" She seemed nervous as if she didn't want to know the answer, and he could have sworn her teeth were chattering.

"I … I took a walk, read a little." He tried to appear casual.

"What did you read?"

"The paper."

Frowning, she spun around in anger. "David, it was still on the porch when I came in."

David followed her, catching the frame of the door before it slammed on him. "I read one while I was out … I went out."

She was suspicious, her eyes darting around the kitchen as if some evidence would prove him right or wrong, but then relented. "All right. Sorry. Sounds good to me. I'm … ah, glad for you."

David laid his palms on the countertop and pressed himself to her. They hadn't made love since he was on vacation, technically speaking. Julia didn't back away. He kissed her on the lips.

David's back was sore. He told Julia he needed to stretch it outside, and immediately sensed her frustration. "It's the only place where I won't get stepped on or fall on some toys."

He lay back down on the grass he regarded as a separate address from the one on the front door, and made his body long and slim like a pencil with his arms up over his head, elbows in. He felt invisible and watched the clouds moving, changing colour as they did so, an eggshell white to dull grey. A quarter moon stationed itself over the left side of the roof. He thought about the places on earth where it was dark for months of the year and light for other months. *One would never know when to end the day or when to start it*, he thought. He had the urge to consult the astronomy website Ellen used for her project and check how time would be calculated if he lived on another planet. When his parents had taken him to Nova Scotia to visit Gloria and her family when they lived up there, the summer fields extended in front of him like an endless land of thin bones. He had dreamt of being buried underground, suffocating under the weight of the stalks. The thick air, constantly perfumed, had been difficult to overcome, especially since Gloria's child, Will, lent him his old bike so they could ride all day. They went to the bay and watched as crabs and lobster were lifted to shore in huge nets, creature crushed against creature, clicking in fright. It rained for five days straight. He'd never seen such unrelenting rain. It knocked him off the bike once. Then, too, he was constantly asking the time and when it would be over. Gloria had taught them how to play cards. His father and mother played against Gloria and Uncle Craig and the sense of suffocation dragged on with every round.

"David, honey?"

"What? ... where?" He saw white spots in front of his eyes like headlights. "I think you fell asleep."

"Julia?"

"I said I think you fell asleep. Come on inside."

David could feel the gentle nudge of an arm, and a hand circling fingers within his. The spots disappeared, and he saw Julia leaning beside him. He desperately wished to follow her, and, yet, the thought of sleeping in his bedroom panicked him.

"Why don't you sleep out here with me?"

Julia paused, visibly taken aback. He knew she'd hidden the handcuffs, and he knew it was probably for the best though he resented her a little for it. He needed a logical explanation for not going back inside. The kids had already watched the movie, and, because it was a school night, would probably be asleep in the next hour.

"It's lovely out here, Jules. Really. When was the last time you even sat and looked up at the stars?"

"We can't see stars here, David."

"Sure you can." He gave her a clownish smile. "Well, even if you can't. It's still nice. Better than pictures of them."

Julia took David's other hand and smoothed each of the fingers individually. "Are you sure you're feeling better? That you're not ... oh ..." She held tighter, scratching her fingernail across one of his. "I work in a hospital ... and ..."

"I want to be outside, that's all." He sighed. "Is it unhealthy to be outdoors, Nurse?"

"Just tell me this handcuff thing is going to end, David."

"I'm all right, don't worry," David replied.

Julia sighed. "One second then."

Julia unfolded two white plastic lawn chairs and brought them down from the patio.

"Sitting position satisfactory?" she asked, getting settled.

"I think so," David answered and followed suit, wrapping his arms around the back of the chair, one hand holding on to the high leg. A few minutes of silence moved around them like fog.

"You're right, you know," Julia offered. "It is quite lovely to be outside today." She stared at her garden through the dark, the pink faces of roses protruding under the back light. She rose and plucked one, twirling it in her hand and pacing the lawn casually. "Have you thought about the house at all?"

David shook his head in the negative.

"I have ... and I'm pretty torn, I guess," she said, dropping loose petals through her fingers. "I love this house ... but, you know, I also really love your parents' house. Out of the city, where we can actually see the stars. Maybe we could rent it until the kids finish high school or ... I don't know ... I've just been thinking."

David nodded in the affirmative. Julia dropped the stem. "I'm going to bed. I don't want to find you out here in the morning, okay? Promise?"

David promised.

At 3:00 a.m. David removed the handcuffs he had found earlier in the cutlery drawer and started his car. He could recall this place on the drive out to his old house, where he grew up, that would rent him a canoe for the day. It would only take a few hours of driving to reach it. He was in the same clothes he had on two days ago, but he felt refreshed and left Julia a loving note. *When do I get a rest?* his mother had written when she'd asked David to put his father in a home. *I've been thinking of going to Florida to visit Gloria. I could use the sun, don't you think?* David had agreed. He had even paid for her flight. David pulled out of the driveway as unobtrusively as he could. He knew what he wanted to do with the last day of his vacation. He wanted to take that canoe out as far as he could row, and, no matter what, he wanted to make his way back to shore.

Blind Spot

The Two-Timing Bastard turned left onto Church Street, parked the Ford, and entered the Shoppers Drug Mart. She wanted to follow him but hadn't packed her wig, and she was still awaiting alterations on her new spring coat. She had decided to stick with the car today, and he usually didn't make stops. Now she would have to wait, so she turned on the radio and ate a Butterfinger chocolate bar from the stash she shoved into the glove compartment.

When the Son of a Bitch emerged, she threw the candy wrapper out the window. He was carrying a long white plastic shopping bag that appeared to contain an eight-roll package of toilet paper, two rolls protruding from the top of the handles. She could not detect the brand through the coloured slogan of the drugstore, but imagined it was the one on sale in the front window. She nearly screamed and hit the rental car pedals as hard as she could. The car was in park and the only damage done was to her ankles. As she cursed her cheap heels and her own inadequacy at never having learned to kick properly, the Rat slipped her sight. Restarting the car, she mumbled about toilet paper under her breath. Is he going to wipe her ass for her?

she asked the window shield. Look at the Loser with his balding sweaty head and blue uniform jacket. Just look at him out on the streets and in his car on his way to meet his lady love!

She barely slowed down at the stop sign, even though she knew the woman lived at the Sky Pro apartment building on Jarvis Street, an area she'd never frequented until this last month of spying. Still, she kept three car-lengths away from the grey Ford with the familiar licence plate. Three weeks ago her fingers had lingered on the telephone pad as she decided whether or not she wanted to claim the vehicle had been stolen. She had the whole scene worked out: the police cruiser finding the car at Slut's place, the fumbling explanations as he tried to clear up the misunderstanding with the authorities, and, of course, the profuse apologies later as she feigned shock. I was worried sick about you, she'd say, her fingernails gripping the sofa chair for balance. Many tears would be shed, and only she the wiser. But she decided it was important to keep a certain distance, at least for now. She didn't want to catch him before she was ready. She would confront him, but needed to pick the right time for the scene. A scene like the ones she had witnessed in restaurants or shopping mall food courts where dinner rolls flew across tables and hair was pulled, where handbags became weapons and drinks were tossed like acid into stunned eyes. They didn't shop together and went to restaurants so rarely that she always wanted dessert. One couldn't cause a real scene after eating chocolate cheesecake. The mood was wrong and her stomach would be bulging.

Because there is very little free parking on Jarvis Street, she circled the building three times before returning the car, having told the attendant hers was in the shop and she was afraid of subways, what with all the suicides, and not too long ago the story of a man who pushed a woman in front of a car because he couldn't find a job. At least Scumbag had a job, although he'd worked for the delivery service for the last twenty-five years and had only received one minuscule promotion. That was right after they were married and she had phoned her mother proudly to tell the Nosy Witch she had been wrong for once. He wasn't lazy. He was just unimpressive, probably stupid, too. At least he had seniority and a health plan. They'd saved a lot of money through the years, although the child benefits had gone completely to waste.

She knew the woman's name, or at least her surname. Ms. Fisher. Of course she's a Ms., she had laughed. Aren't all Mss. tricky ladies with time on their hands? Clever, oh, very clever, she imagined. A woman with a hidden past and a pink canopy bed and an enigmatic voice on her answering machine: *Please leave a message, I so wish to hear from you.* One day she even saw her. Someone had called out to her because the Bitch dropped a letter from her mailbox. "Ms. Fisher," the young gentleman said, reading the inscription, "I think this is yours." Ms. Fisher wore a scarf around her neck, a lavender rayon scarf, not unlike one she herself sometimes wore. Immediately, she ascertained the woman had strange tastes.

Figuring she had a couple of hours before the Asshole returned to their semi-detached postwar home on the upper east side of Toronto, she took the subway without fear down to Union Station. She'd heard on a radio call-in show that you could meet successful and eligible men near Union; all the bank towers were located there, and the Sony Centre seated the crème de la crème every night of the week. She chose the darkly lit restaurant across from the theatre in which to sit, wearing her good black suit jacket and skirt, well-kept as she wore them only to funerals, with a tight silk green blouse. A man with tickets to the ballet couldn't be a deliveryman. A woman in a tight silk green blouse couldn't be a bookkeeper married to a deliveryman. She'd never attended the ballet or opera. Anyone, she begged the straw in her drink, anyone but a deliveryman who brings his mistress toilet paper would be a fine catch. Her virgin Bloody Mary tasted like straight tomato juice, and she nibbled nervously on the complimentary cheese sticks and assorted nuts, checking the door and her watch when she sensed noise or movement. Today would be different, she told herself, than the other attempts. She didn't know if she would go so far as to make a hotel date or slip into the back of a man's car, especially since when she went to the washroom she realized she was wearing cotton full-waisted briefs with a tiny hole on one side, but at least she could tease out a phone number and keep it in the pocket of her slacks, ready the next time the Half-Assed Moron left their house.

Sometimes, like today, she brought a book. Not one of her ledgers, but a book selected from the bestsellers shelves at the bookstore in the small shopping plaza near her home. Mostly she purchased spy novels or murder mysteries. She didn't read them — she liked non-fiction biographies better, her favourites about politicians and their secret lives, but thought they might make her look like a lonely admirer of the rich and famous. Spy novels and murder mysteries had more interesting covers. They needed to look intelligent, but not too serious; exciting, but not over-dramatic; and they had to be paperbacks. She couldn't bear dog-earing hardcover books, and then how would anyone believe she was reading? Her book today was called *The Seasoned Traveller*, with an opaque black cover featuring a passport photograph of a woman in shades and perfectly arched dark eyebrows. The headline read, "A stunning read — you won't put it down," so she leaned against the brass bar counter as if hypnotized. She started on page 130: *After turning the corner and leaving the car, Ameila Bronzeheart could sense the smell of a man behind her....* She placed her leather bookmark to the right of her mauve cocktail napkin. Once in a while she looked up, smiled, and stirred her drink.

Later at home, she folded that morning's laundry and cursed herself for being such an idiot. The Pig had his fat face glued to the television and didn't notice her muttering as she divided the clothes into homogenous piles. A handsome man, younger than herself she might add, had asked to buy her a drink. He wore a navy blue two-piece suit and a silk red tie with a gold lapel pin. He was well-groomed with a full head of grey, distinguished hair. Their smiles met. *Stupid! Stupid! Stupid!* When she opened her mouth to accept his offer, without her consent it blurted out: "I'm married." He said he didn't mind, it was just a drink and some chat if she wanted to take a break from her book before the show started. Yes, she wanted to. Definitely. "I'm sorry," she said again. "I'm married." Then she settled her bill, which thankfully didn't list that she was drinking a virgin Bloody Mary, and boarded the subway home. The switching television channels hurt her eyes, so she got up to fold the rest of the Waste's shirts in their bedroom, dreaming about how different things would be if she were folding suits and silk ties instead of polyester sleeves and jumpsuits.

After the Brute's breakfast the next morning, she walked down to the street to visit her friend Fran. Fran had a seventeen-year-old boy who used to cut their lawn a few summers ago for spending money. *Maybe he would do,* she mused, a little guilty at picking on one of her friends. But she was desperate, and all was fair in love and war, she told herself. She knocked, explained what she needed from Fran's son, and the matter was settled between them. They sat down to a cup of tea and exchanged rumours about the divorced woman who lived next door and the workmen adding an addition to her house. Neither of them had done anything to theirs, except minor necessary repairs. They talked about paint jobs, curtains, and a friendly open-concept kitchen. They laughed themselves silly imitating the East-Indian couple three doors down who aired their dirty laundry on the street without the least semblance of shame. Last week, the husband had accused the wife of spending his paycheque on a new washing machine when the old one, when he had time to fix it, would last another twenty years. He tore down the laundry she had put up on the line, and she began jumping up and down on his clothes. After an hour, the women parted ways.

She knew the Bottom Feeder's usual routine. The Sky Pro apartment building was on his afternoon route. She wondered how he had met Ms. Fisher, considering the packages he delivered were generally to businesses. He would have been delivering to the Sky Pro superintendent or one of the three stores on the ground floor, and not to one of the residents. A dropped letter for Ms. Fisher, perhaps. A held-open door. The possibilities were few, and yet she couldn't really imagine them fully in her mind. The Freak didn't know how to talk to women. He'd pee his own pants rather than come up with a pick-up line. Ms. Fisher must have started the conversation. Maybe, at first, she'd wanted something very simple from him: help with her groceries or a match to light a cigarette. Surely, she'd needed to speak to him for a reason. The Dumpster wasn't a handsome man.

The day's travels were uninformative. He delivered his packages, ate the ham-and-cheese sandwich and Granny Smith apple lunch she'd packed him, and delivered more packages. He remained at Sky Pro for only twenty minutes. Enough for a quickie, but she didn't think so. He would hate to crumple his uniform. She supposed they just talked. But about what? All he'd done was deliver packages and eat lunch. What could he possibly be telling her but lies? Her wig, stuffed in her handbag, lay there waiting for the right mood, and she was feeling sleepy.

After a nap, she got ready, splashing on some perfume and then deciding against it. She curled her hair with an iron, and tried to fix the split ends left over from a bad permanent. Cover-up was dabbed on top of the oval wrinkles under her pale blue eyes and the curled dents near her mouth. Next she tweezed a couple of straggling blonde hairs under her chin. Talcum powder was pressed under her armpits, and a light lipstick used to fill out her thin lips. Then she squeezed into a purple wool skirt and a white satin blouse buttoned all the way to the top of her neck. *No need to push things too far*, she had decided. *He is only a boy, after all.*

She descended the stairs and found the envelope of coupons she kept beside the telephone in the kitchen. The doorbell rang. She flashed the Back Stabber a brutal sneer behind his balding head as he watched television. *At least I have the decency to look good when I go out with the opposite sex*, she prided herself.

"Hello, Jake, come on in." She gestured with a full-toothed smile. "I just need to grab my purse." She returned to the kitchen and faked checking around for it. She could hear Jake speaking to His Sloppiness.

"Mrs. Lockwood told my mother she needed help at the grocery store. Something about the car." He was leaning against the sofa as he spoke, trying to decipher what program was on.

The Large Fart grunted his assent.

Mrs. Lockwood took the boy's arm with a motherly grace and headed out, pretending she lost her grip on the door handle so that it slammed. *He doesn't give a shit*, she stormed inwardly. The Couch Potato wasn't even paying attention. Jake opened the passenger side door for her, as if by habit instead of any intention to be polite, but she blushed despite herself.

At the store, as Jake helped her gather fruits and vegetables, slabs of meat from the deli counter, and assorted cans of soups and dips, he told her about his high school and his new girlfriend. The girl in question was two years younger than him and she asked if he ever thought of dating an older woman. Oh, he replied, his last girlfriend was a year older, but he didn't like it very much, and her friends didn't get along with his friends. Besides, the new girl was prettier and liked the same movies. He moved with a lanky surety, a coy softness that made her nostalgic for her own teenage years. She remembered necking once with a boy who resembled him with his slightly dishevelled oak-brown hair and his complimentary eyes, a long red-and-green rugby shirt covering the zipper of his jeans. She'd told the young man who looked like Jake not to go too far with her, because she wanted to be with him forever. They lasted three weeks; she'd never taken off her panties for him and regretted it, crying against her mother's shoulder, unable to confess that he was the first boy to touch her newly budded breasts. She was sure, however, that Jake had already managed to get into this new girlfriend's panties. Several times.

They polished off the list in an hour, and he helped her carry the packages and drove her home. At the driveway, she handed him a twenty-dollar bill.

"Oh, no, Mrs. Lockwood. I can't take money from you."

She stared at him, the woman who came to have tea with his mother once a week, his new muscles underneath his shirt aching to get to the movies and have oral sex in the dark with his prettier girlfriend. She didn't like not to pay him, especially with the tone of his voice, as if she were a grandmother or an invalid and not a vivacious woman who had puffed out the waist of her blouse to hide the fleshy belly smile she had developed over the years, who had taken pains to wear the higher-heeled shoes that showed off her calves.

"No. I insist. I might need you again," she countered. "That car is so old I can't trust it anymore."

Taking the money, he drove away with a flippant but pleasant wave. She brought the last of the plastic bags in by herself, and, when safe in the kitchen, wiped her lipstick off with a tissue.

"He's such a nice boy, isn't he?" she called to the Worm.

"Sure," he said. "Fran's kid, right?"

"Uh-huh."

When she finished putting the groceries away and stashing the plastic bags underneath the sink to recycle as garbage bags, she slouched beside the Fungus on the couch, sliding off her heels and pulling out the ends of her blouse from the band of her skirt. The wool was beginning to irritate her. He was watching *Wheel of Fortune*, exhibiting no interest in the outcome. The Blank Head wasn't even guessing at the answers.

"Yeah."

"Yeah." She sighed as the woman in the middle called out her answer. "He does pretty well with the ladies, Fran tells me. I was lucky he was free tonight."

"Oh ya." He didn't take his eyes off the screen.

"A real heart-breaker. So good-looking and healthy. Bright, too. Any girl would be happy to have him, wouldn't they?" she prodded as Pat Sajak escorted the same happy woman to the bonus round.

"Probably."

"Does he get any love letters?"

"Huh?"

"Love letters."

He turned to face her. "You know I don't deliver anything like that. This isn't even my neighbourhood."

"I know. I was just teasing," she answered flatly, upset at herself now that she was actually interested in whether or not the woman would win the grand prize and go off on an exotic trip to Peru or drive home in a brand-new Porsche.

"Oh." He took her hand in his and squeezed, his eyes

wandering back to the flashing lights. The woman lost, but seemed placated by her previous winnings, clapping and waving into the camera. She stayed on the sofa for most of the evening and they watched the television together, once in a while touching hands. She wanted to kill him.

For the next few days she lay low, hiding out at home, doing chores. Her stash of Butterfingers was moved to the medicine cabinet, which housed cough syrup, some allergy pills, but was otherwise dusty and neglected. *Let him wonder why I'm always in the bathroom*, she thought, covering the wrappers with toilet paper before tossing them in the wastebasket. *Maybe he'll think I'm pregnant.* She chuckled. And it was she who hadn't wanted children. He never begged her or anything, wasn't capable of such a display of dramatics, but he'd brought it up a few times over the years and she'd said no. Firmly. She didn't want to be one of those women changing diapers and wiping noses all day. But later it was she who asked, and he'd looked annoyed at her, then in her late thirties, as if to say, *"So you think you're young now?"* Her hair had already been turning grey for a number of years. He had already started seeing a proctologist. Who was she kidding? But she knew it was possible to still have children. Even in her mid-forties she heard there were things that could be done, and she asked him that night.

"Do you ever wonder what it would have been like if we'd had kids?" She stood at the dresser, wearing a long white dressing gown on top of flannel underwear, pulling bobby pins out of her hair, and clipping them onto a cardboard strip.

"Makes no sense to wonder now," he said, wiping his forehead with a blue handkerchief he kept on his side of the bed, and rolled over.

She let her hair fall, a streak of grey peeking out from behind her neck that she had trouble reaching with her home dye kit. *Makes no sense to him.* She sighed inwardly. *That house hasn't been on his route for a while.*

Two days later, in the afternoon, she put on her wig. She picked a synthetic one, almost black, close to a dark stormy grey, which seemed natural enough and innocuous in its simplicity. It was also easy to put on and take off, with a strong plastic net woven into the skull that fitted snugly just underneath the widow's peak of her own hair. The lady at The Bay was attentive, probably perceiving from the outset that she was going to make a sale. She even told her why she was buying it, not caring what a complete stranger knew, even a little curious to discover what one would think.

"I'm going to spy on my husband."

"Okay," she said, adjusting the hair and angling her face towards the three-way mirror behind her. "You'd be surprised how many times I hear that."

"Really?" It wasn't that strange, was it? There were probably millions of cheating bastards helping out the wig economy.

"Sure. There are lots of reasons people buy wigs," she answered carelessly, as if she were listing off favourite colours. "Some want to spy on someone, some want a new life and think a new hairdo will help, and some, you know, it's not their choice, really. I've got lots of cancer patients, and even a few of those people who are so nervous they can't stop tearing out their hair. It's a disease."

"Pretty sad, isn't it?"

"Sometimes. And sometimes you make people happy." The clerk shrugged pleasantly. She had a childishness to her, though it was apparent in her stout legs and saggy neck that she was older by a few years at least; yet her manner was delicate, as if she were laying out silk gloves or stockings, and her voice was tuned cheerfully like a music box.

The wig was a perfect fit. It was thick, full-bodied, and curled uniformly around the shoulders. A full head of hair, one might say, in an attractive bob. She thought the clerk was wearing one herself, with its perfect shine under the lights of the booth, but didn't think it would be polite to ask.

"You need one with bangs," she said. "Your husband might know you from your forehead. You'd be surprised what they recognize."

My forehead, she thought. Well, who knew where he looked when they deigned to have sex anymore. Maybe it was her forehead with the thick night cream that cost thirty dollars and promised tighter, younger-looking skin in weeks. Maybe he would recognize the smell of her forehead if not its shape. The clerk fitted one the same colour and length as the other, but now with bangs.

"Yes. Yes. The shoulder-curl really works."

"In case he knows my neck. Right?"

"Exactly."

They giggled like schoolgirls.

"It's funny. From what I've heard and seen," the clerk added, "at home you could walk around with Christmas lights strapped to your head and they won't even think to ask if you've done something new with your hair. But when they don't know you're around, husbands are always drawn to women who resemble their wives."

Mrs. Lockwood, alias Husband-Spyer, left The Bay clerk a hefty tip.

Appearing in public with the wig on, she thought she looked a few years younger, or perhaps mildly eccentric. Dark glasses and a new beige taffeta scarf, her own hair pinned up, flattened and hidden, she felt like one of the actresses in her celebrity biographies, off to a secret rendezvous or trying to outwit her fans. The clerk insisted no one would be able to tell she was wearing a wig, except a child. Try not to pass by schools or playgrounds, she advised. Apparently, children always know if someone's in disguise. Smart. Or else maybe adults instinctively accept it. *One of life's strange mysteries*, she thought, and ate another Butterfinger in her rented car.

Back out on the prowl, she soon spotted his Ford, *their* Ford, thank you very much, at the mail outlet. He was picking up parcels. Maybe today there would be a change in pace. Teeth clenched, he carried the bundles back to the car from the back garage, sweat glistening on his forehead, his jumpsuit legs rubbing together as he took short blunt steps. She watched him out of her rear-view mirror, parked on the road. He circled the driveway and passed her, doing the speed limit. She shoved the last piece of chocolate into her mouth and shadowed behind.

When he made a stop at the hardware store near Ms. Fisher's, she parked and followed him inside. A large burly man in a red uniform asked her if she needed assistance and she lost him. She shook the clerk off, claiming that she'd call him when she did need some, and he retreated behind his counter. In the concave mirror, meant to catch shoplifters, she spotted the Blob. It appeared he was there to buy a screwdriver, picking up one and then another in the third aisle, inspecting the tips. Her heartbeat sped up and she felt her hands grow cool and sweaty as she found her way to the aisle, then pretended to be interested in the various packages of nails not five feet from where he stood. She could smell him, the thin film of dust from the garage mixed with the sweat of lifting and tin scent of the store. Surprised and disgusted with herself, she was aroused. *The rush of my blood must be doing this to my body*, she told herself. *If the expensive musk cologne of the gentleman from the Sony restaurant could not entice me, then certainly this labour odour from the ordinary man I've slept against for the last twenty-five years wouldn't do the trick.* But there she was in the hardware store, a pleasant pain pushing against her pelvis. If she wanted, she could take her left arm out of her coat pocket and touch him, or at least touch the square-tipped metal screwdriver in his hand.

Standing there, a package of framing nails in her left hand, the burly man returned and asked her if she was all right. In all the excitement and dizziness, she'd lost him. Removing her shades, she tried to get a closer look at the front of the store where the tiny bell sounded off not a few seconds before. He was nowhere to be seen, and the smell of him had disappeared.

"I think I need these," she said, as if stunned.

The burly man took them from her outstretched palm and directed her toward the cash register.

"You can always bring them back if they're not the right ones. Just keep the receipt."

"Sure you can," she said, stuffing the nails into her purse. "I'll do just that."

Not caring if the burly man saw her, she stripped the wig off her head, walked out the door, and threw it in the garbage bin outside. She didn't even indulge in thoughts of what he might be fixing with the brand-new screwdriver at Ms. Fisher's. She drooped in her car and sped home.

The next day, after saying goodbye to the Waste Case, she took the subway to the main intersection near Jarvis Street. After lingering outside the coffee shop on the ground floor of the Sky Pro apartments, sipping a large black coffee and dipping one of her Butterfingers, she ventured inside. Sporting the lavender scarf that was similar to Ms. Fisher's, she was fumbling with her purse to appear distracted, when a man with a key to the foyer of the apartment building called to her.

"You live in the building, right?"

"Ah, yes. I'm just having trouble finding my key." He held the door ajar with his back, and then halted the elevator before it closed.

"Thank you. I'll just sit here and dump it out before I go up." The doors erased him.

Nice man, she thought. *Trusting.* One thing out of the way, she concentrated next on the apartment number she had read on the board. Fourteen-o-five. Inside the elevator, she jangled her car keys in her coat pocket, wishing she'd stashed herself another chocolate bar.

The fourteenth floor was covered in a pinkish-beige short-haired carpet. She slunk down the hallway, until she came face to face with fourteen-o-five, the door of Ms. Fisher's apartment, and, noticing no one, pressed her cheek against the door. The faint hum of a Billie Holiday song escaped through the wood. *I like that song*, she thought, then held her breath and knocked.

A middle-aged woman appeared in brown slacks and a dull, long-sleeved yellow sweater like the kind her mother used to knit. She wore little makeup, a bit of black eyeliner and blue shadow on her lids, and a peach lipstick with a matte finish. Her eyes, once they ascertained no recognition for the woman at the door, centred pleasingly upon her scarf.

"I'm not in need of anything," she said tentatively.

"I'm not selling anything."

"No?"

"No. I'm … I'm Mrs. Lockwood."

Ms. Fisher retreated a single step back into her apartment corridor.

"I suppose you would like to come in," she said.

"I would."

"All right," she said.

"Then you'll need to move away from the door."

"Oh, yes. I guess I will," Ms. Fisher replied, stepping inside.

Mrs. Lockwood entered the apartment, and, taking off her coat and boots, followed Ms. Fisher into the living room.

While tea brewed, Mrs. Lockwood was disappointed to find furnishings as bland and lower middle-class as her own. The door to her bedroom was ajar and there was no pink canopy bed in sight, just a standard wooden frame and matching dressers. Fake daffodils were arranged in a clear glass vase in the centre of the coffee table and the rugs were all an off-white colour. On the television unit were three picture frames, two of graduation photos, a boy and a girl, and one a family portrait, the kind done in department stores with a cloudy blue background. The man in the photo looked tired and Ms. Fisher, a decade ago, apprehensive. The children wore goofy grins mired in that awkward stage between childhood and adolescence when none of their features have adequately settled. Between the photos, tiny ceramic figurines, one of an elephant, another of a child, and a third of a black kitten, radiated the air of gifts from friends who'd gone on trips and had not known what to bring back for her.

"My name's Joan," Ms. Fisher offered as she brought out the tea pot, a cup of sugar, and some milk, and sat in a brown upholstered chair close to the couch.

"Helen."

"I don't have cream," she added. "I'm sorry, I usually just steam milk for mine."

"I'm the same way," Helen replied with a hint of intimacy that surprised her.

She stirred her tea and smoothed her dress with her hands.

Priscila Uppal

"I guess we should talk," Joan said, crossing her legs.

"We probably should," Helen replied, nodding sadly.

And after a few minutes, with the comfort of hot tea and the familiar surroundings of the apartment, neither of the women could tell to whom any of this belonged.

COVER BEFORE STRIKING

The most common phrase in the world in print is *Cover Before Striking*. Thousands of books with tiny cardboard flaps in every language telling the same story, the same lie. It's madness to think, with all the warnings, no one seems to be listening.

every language telling the same story

Crazy was a word my father used a lot, especially in association with women. Women were invented to create havoc for men, my father said. Fire-eaters. Looking to cause trouble where there doesn't need to be any. Set fire to your pants and then to your house. That's what women do. You would nod and make faces. I would say nothing, until later, in my bed, when he would rub my belly and ask those questions. I would have to answer. Crazy. Irrational, if he felt like being more psychological about it. Those things never happened. You made them up. You're always telling stories. You are lying.

a word my father used a lot

Lying crazy on your living room floor. Burgundy carpet burned, frayed, pink spots from vodka spills, keeps my back warm, tickling like fur on my knees. Yellow plastic ashtray bought at the discount store in the market, Made in Taiwan. You laughed and said we were all Made in Taiwan. And I imagined myself being melted into a shape with grooves for sticks and fingers to fit. With small black type across my back and ashes smeared on my face. Watch the smoke curl and rise like runaway clouds in a storm, afraid of catching the fever, paper burning in staircase spirals the way I thought fairytale houses would, filter glowing like a pulsating wound, flicking my lighter on and off, on and off, each crack from my fingertips making me tremble. Intoxication. Your feet dangle over my hair, wide and black spread on red. Yellow light telling me to slow down. Slow down. The dizzy feeling in my belly, the downtown traffic. Gazing at the ceiling, dripping the last swig of vodka onto my thighs to mix with your come. My grooves sore but aching for your fingers. I am lost in the smoke.

curl and rise like runaway clouds

He would smile when he said it. Dark thinning hair without a part. Bushy eyebrows furled in amusement. Lips a tense bow. Arms like pendulums. I never knew which side he was going to take. Swing. Swing. I wanted to hit him. Make the movement stop. Take his balding head in my shaking hands and beat it on our yellow fridge, watch the magnets (mushroom, doctor's number, pizza place, preschool blushing heart), watch them fall to the floor like exploding stars and the picture I had drawn three years earlier, still up on the fridge because no one paid attention, curled at the corners, smudged with fingerprints, grease from cooking, frying our food always in too much oil. Everything we ate in shades of brown or black, burnt bread and fried, trying to disguise the smell with fans whirling, whirling smoke and ashes all over the kitchen, beating the alarm with a broom handle to stop the wailing, wailing, announcing our food was overcooked, overdone, again. Stashing the broom in the crack between the fridge and cupboard. I wanted that lilac to fall. All other flowers wilt. I wanted to press his face up against it, beat him with the broom handle I'd felt on my back, my back, and lower than that. Make him bleed. See I was still a child three years ago drawing with Crayolas, sometimes unable to stay inside the lines.

all other flowers wilt

Dinnertime. I am tired of mashed potatoes and peas, green and white mush served in sterile silence. Only sometimes a smile from the pretty nurse, the one with long raven black hair feathered like crows' wings, brushed back into a silver pin that glitters under the blinds. I want to feel her hair and have her feed me with her large spoon like a child. I usually accept another helping to watch her move, row by row. I know I could've been a nurse like her. I like to think she could've been me.

Dinnertime

Smile, you said. You're such a sorry drunk. Good fuck, considering, but stop being so sad. And don't look up at me like that. You know it's true. Show me your tits. Come on. I'm just teasing. Have another beer. Take a toke. I got more. We can get more if you want. Just stop lying there being sad. We could play a game. We could get under those covers again. We could smoke up more afterwards. What do you think? What game would you like to play this time?

don't look up at me like that

Cover Before Striking

We played the thermostat game daily. Behind your eyes I'd sneak and sweat, aware of your body lying somewhere on the other side of the wall, risking getting caught to see if we could steal more heat. Hiding in blankets. Rolling ourselves into balls. Breathing into each other's hands. It never felt warmer, but the rising thermometer told me I'd won. I'd stolen something from you. It was enough.

aware of your body lying somewhere

12 was not as attractive as 13. 13 wasn't quite as sophisticated as 14. And 16 was where I wanted to be kissing boys in alleys, getting felt up. Until of course 18 when you've done all that and it's old hat. Childish. You are beginning to do it well now, with rhythm. You know what makes you feel up instead of being felt up.

16 was where I wanted to be

Up there, he said, pointing with his skinny arms to the planet he is going to save. Up is where you go when you die. Past the airplanes and the clouds. That's why I'm going to save it. Past the moon? I ask. Past everything. This house. This street. Your school. You get to get out of here and play. I am going to be a hero. I thought my brother was very wise. Will you take me with you? I asked.

Up is where you go when

The telephone was black with white numbers, the rotary kind that clicked while the dial spun, plotting each number like Morse code. Click, click, click. Under the door I barred with my dresser and rocking chair, feet hooked to the vent. My huge wooden dresser with the white lamb painted on the drawers. Tiny balloon labels to proclaim what was inside. Miscellaneous on the one that kept my writings, aligning myself with knickknacks and old candy wrappers, yelling that I was calling Children's Aid. I saw it as a flashing red siren sign like the ones in front of hospitals and emergency medical clinics, ambulances and fire trucks roaring in, a large man sweeping me up in his arms and carrying me off like a baby down a long white ladder as flames flew out the windows, fireworks exploding on the lawn, the man cradling my limbs and singing me a lullaby, telling me to fall asleep, asleep, the red truck crying with me, saying I wasn't going crazy, I would be okay, I would never have to see the house again. You yelling back that you didn't care. They would never believe a nine-, ten-, twelve-year-old girl over her own father. They would know I was just a wacko, troublemaker, fire-eater, slut seeking attention. They'd take a picture so they'd have my number next time around and bring me right back. Knuckles in mid-dial, I'd put down the receiver, believing you. You were so large and strong telling me no one else would take care of me. I'd move the furniture, crawl back into bed, and cry, once again, for forgiveness.

Click, click, click

It is too quiet here. My men parading around, bumping into me, moody, moody men roaming inside of me. Waking up, making breakfasts, on the phone, in the shower, moving the pictures around, rearranging the cupboards. Where did you go? Why have you returned to live here, mute and waving? Why do you screech in my ears only when I'm trying to sleep? When I am wanting to wish you good night?

My men parading around, bumping

Take me back to the old neighbourhood, tired bungalows all lined up like cigarettes in a pack, the smell of tarred driveways, the crooked street sign. Ashbrook Crescent. No brook, no pond, just a long curvy street with children playing road hockey, me with my arm in another cast on the sidelines saving worms from the grates and the tires, moving them into camps, slime-covered fingers, the autumn leaves raked into piles to be swept away, dumped into the garbage, even though everyone thinks they're pretty before they fall. Every year the dumpster would catch fire and we would gather around broken gravel and watch the huge green box glow like an abandoned planet, the thick fumes of burnt leaves rustling over the streets, confetti in red, black, yellow, green, dripping and rising in the wind, landing to be buried in a new place, secret messages scattered along the highways and boulevards and our crescent, too, forgotten and crumpled, unread, burning. Car!, the kids wail and join me on the sidewalk for a few seconds then back to the game. Jersey sweatshirts, hats, belonging to a team, a city, the world, much more than this Ashbrook Crescent without so much as a fire hydrant.

join me on the sidewalk for a few seconds

Cover Before Striking

You wouldn't let me light your cigarettes anymore. I burnt your eyebrows. I missed your eyes.

I burnt your eyebrows

Pyromaniac. I loved the word when I first heard it. Elated when the doctor told me that's what I was. Finally I know. Heat and smoke, the stench of ash, hypnotic effect of light caught in a pure bursting bubble of destruction. This is me. This is who I love. If you don't stop, they will put you away. Put you in a new place. Re-place you. Maniacs are easy to find.

the doctor told me that's what I was

Cover Before Striking

I poured lighter fluid from the Zippo all over them. I didn't want to see the stains from my blood, crusty red rusty reminders of you, sex, the thick smell like fog, if you turn it's overwhelming, your sweat and mine in patches, spills, on the bedsheets, the pin-striped blue sheets. I burned them all. They found me passed out, drunk, matches clasped to my hands, ashes rubbed over my limbs. Man's first invention.

your sweat and mine in patches

You came home without taking a shower. Did you think I couldn't smell her sex on your face as you brushed by to make coffee? It didn't smell like your waitress friend. The redhead with the long fake fingernails, a broken one I found in your suit pocket. A new one. A replacement. My body cold and frigid to your touch. Evenings spent picturing you undressing her. Slow. Calculating. Silk black stockings slipping off like drops of water down a glass, hanging from a chair as you pound into her. Hard and hungry. Your body I know, I can read as Braille, each indentation marking spaces where you live and breathe without me. No more grooves. No more fingers. No more. I'd wonder if your body moved the same way it did with me. First slow like a reptile, scaly and slick, and then quicker, forceful, until you'd bite the side of my armpit and come, your head, neck stretched, past me on the bed, past all of me, holding out for that moment of release, collapsing sweat wet kisses in my hair, holding you like a child at my breast, my thighs red, rough red, red. Did she do that for you? Did she do more? I never asked. I only know her by the smell and the guilty look in your eyes.

like a child at my breast, my thighs

Cover Before Striking

Colours, colours, all the beautiful colours, hues pure, pure, like fireworks, green, yellow, purple, blue pages burnt and blowing away, up, up, up, my diary destroying itself, taking back all those words, all those lies.

all the beautiful colours

They like it when I write here. They don't read it of course. But they like my hands to be busy. They always want to see where our hands are.

when I write here. They don't

My favourite memory of you. One night I broke like the thermo-stat and couldn't stop melting, though I was cold, cold. Holding my knees, rocking back and forth in the apartment, the television wouldn't stop blinking, my moody men trapped inside reporting the news, solving crimes, waking the dead. Stop, I cried. Stop it right now. You got out the thick camping blanket, the red and black plaid one, and wrapped me up. You carried me outside to the patch of grass by the parking garage. The stars fled, I said. You just can't see them, you said. But they're there. Straddling me gently from behind, holding a glass of water to my lips, kiss-ing my hair. Imagine you're a star, you said, even if no one else can see you. You named a constellation after me, arms encircling me like the Milky Way.

You just can't see them

Priscila Uppal

I learned a soaked pack of matches can be revived if let alone on a sunny day. Though they only spark for a split second. A small atomic bomb.

if let alone on a sunny day

You end all our conversations Take Care. I have been, Father. I always did and now with 400 miles between us you want to check up on me, make sure I'm healthy and happy, not thinking too much or playing with matches, your voice getting shakier as you age. You speak of infections and pills, the nurses, the other men in the home, how you beat them all at chess, such a fine mind you still possess. We tell each other nothing. Nothing we really want to say, like the time you let me cuddle up beside you on the couch and you sang nursery rhymes to me, low monotone voice, inelegant but comforting, black sheep and cockleshells, plums and kidney pies, to put me to sleep, and how you let me win when we arm-wrestled and I would prance around, my arms clenched in fists high, high over my head, Champion of Arm-Wrestling of the World. And how it changed. You found out I kissed a boy in the school clothes closet and you beat me so bad I couldn't walk for days, my guilty lips broken open and chapped, you told my teacher I'd fallen out of a tree. We tell lies, pretend it's all forgotten. Talk about the weather. And sometimes it seems so far away it shouldn't matter anymore and other times the tension in the cord is so electric it is too much for me to bear. Take Care.

arms clenched in fists high

Priscila Uppal

Hang on tight now, and we raced down the hill, my bum bumping on the bicycle seat, the wind stinging my eyes, yelling with delight, go faster, faster, my arms around your waist, go faster, faster, past all the houses, past the cemetery, so fast until we're actually going backwards, back in time, my hair like a kite in the wind, go faster, faster, I know you can, Brother, faster, look back for an instant to wave at those we've left behind.

past all the houses, past the cemetery

Cover Before Striking

Every book of matches has its own story. Date, time, place of purchase, or where I had taken, stolen them from, from whom, and finally what I destroyed neatly labelled on top of the sandpaper striking strip. It was all premeditated. I spoke in tongues. I spoke in tongues.

what I destroyed neatly labelled

I look behind, hearing the sirens, the red trucks arriving, skidding, making no stops, forcing traffic to the sides, men in yellow suits and thick boots like astronauts, holding on at the turn, jumping off, me on the sidewalk watching the smoke rise in black rings into the sky, knowing I was done, I had done it, the frames, ledges, breaking off, falling into pieces, the nosy neighbours leaning out their windows, on the driveway wrapped in winter coats, gawking in gossip horror, on the horn to tell friends about the spectacle, the little girl jumping up and down in the street watching her house burn down, the men running around with their hoses, calling out codes, suited with masks and rubber for protection.

holding on at the turn

Every match a possibility. Every attraction a destruction.

Every

Why? I didn't want to ask him. I didn't know how to put it on.
I don't know. You shaking your head, me embarrassed that my
brother was the only one I could go to and did he know who.
Waiting for the test to finish, in the bathroom, biting nails and
then the relief. That I didn't bring another part of me here. Or
another part of him.

my brother was the only one

Cover Before Striking

I lit the match. Waiting until my fingertips were so hot they were nearly pokers, curling my lips into a kiss and blowing. Wishing the joy wasn't snuffed out so quickly. My fingers snapping open another match.

snapping open another

When the fire alarm goes off here, they all turn toward me. Some start screaming or crying, some don't even blink. The orderlies check if they should bother to take us outside or if it is just a false alarm. There hasn't been a real fire since I arrived. When the alarm goes off though, it is the only time I feel at home.

they all turn toward me

Cover Before Striking

Why do you pronounce fire, fear? you asked once.

you asked

I'm radioactive tonight, you said, and left me yelling your name, standing in the rain. You move so much faster than me, up the street in your long lanky strides, you didn't want to hurt me. Lost like a magician in a puff of smoke. You knowing I hate it when you disappear. Hate crying in public, talking to myself to figure out what's wrong, what voices are speaking to you, if they include mine. Radioactive man, burning me with invisible rays, will you return? There are still planets to save.

you didn't want to hurt me. Lost like

If he loves you, you've won. You're worth something. More than those girls in nylon miniskirts, neon wallflowers at the clubs, scouting for men without rings, or with them if they're successful enough to set you up. Dabbing at your makeup, making passes into mirrors, moving your body to the music to show your rhythms, how your hips can grind, you can make your tits look bigger with the proper bra, or wear none so your nipples stand out under the lights like stars. But if you love him, get ready to make excuses. Because you're working on it. Making it work out. Working on it even if it's so broke it ain't worth holding together with bubblegum and paperclips. If you work on it, it's serious business. Take this love thing and twist it into a box you can fit into. Even if you're just the corner. Even if you're just the lid.

Take this love thing

Priscila Uppal

I would have told you but I wasn't sure how my voice would sound, if it would shake and waver like an expiring flame, falter, make me look guilty, like I was lying. Fire-eater. So I stayed silent, my lips drawn and shut like curtains, you couldn't even guess what was inside the grooves, whose fingers left burn marks on my knees. I didn't want your stories of the clouds and moon to change, so I left you and crawled up the chimney.

stories of the clouds and moon

Cover Before Striking

My mind is too full. The nurses look at me with pity or amusement, I'm not always sure which, my pen scratching wildly on diary pages. Some of you are speaking openly and some of you are so silent I'm beating the words out of you.

pity or amusement

My chest hurts. I can't move my right arm. All the faces and voices flitting around like shadows. You running beside me, calling my name over and over, bending your face into me, keeping up with the speed of the stretcher pushed by four pairs of hands. Lips hot. Cracked. Tears in my mouth. I've done it. Again. Couldn't help it. Lost all feeling in my legs, pressing into the mattress. Sirens singing. A lot of talk. Words. I don't understand. Critical condition. You allowed to come. Drape a blanket. Chin tucks down. I try to wiggle my toes. Shock. You can barely look. I'm sorry. I'm sorry.

A lot of talk

Quiet. They make sure of that. So quiet that my head is a medium where ghosts speak. All my moody men running around now packing suitcases, saying goodbye, slipping through the door and the vents, seeping out of my lungs, ashes on their limbs and eyes, a metronome ticking away over my bed so I know when to eat, when to sleep, when to … The calendar so I know when I will have visitors. When you are here, sitting beside me, I show you diaries and you nod your head and smile and sometimes walk to the barred windows to look at the pretty synthetic garden and I know you feel like crying, but you won't in front of me. This is your duty. See my burnt, twisted hands, red and scarred, as I struggle to grip a spoon or pen. You have another lover and I don't blame you. I enjoy your visits even though I sit straight, immaculately controlled in front of you. Once in a while you sneak me a cigarette. Of course you light it for me and tuck the matches tightly away in your wallet. I sit by the lilac painting as if all the fire is gone from me.

my head is a medium where ghosts

Priscila Uppal

Brother, you stopped telling me stories about the world beyond the skies and stars. I guess we aren't children anymore. I guess we both got out somehow though you never did pedal fast enough to leave, only fast enough not to stop or skid. I still dream of being wrapped around you like a fall jacket and beating the wind and the roads in a ten-speed race. I dream of your olive skin and long bony legs and the way you held a hockey stick like a magic wand and skated circles around me and I giggled in delight to be the centre of the rink so you could pretend you were flying on silver lightning. I dream of your voice, and how I would think you were a hero disguised in blue jeans and a cotton T-shirt who knew all the stories I could never tell.

I dream of your olive skin and long bony legs

Cover Before Striking

A winter fire actually lasts longer than a summer one. It has something to prove.

actually

Priscila Uppal

If I just get it all out, they say I may find some peace. I am trying to let the memories go, give them away to unseen visitors
who may be listening outside the locked doors or behind serving
trays or dancing on my windowsill lighting fires under my feet.
These are my offerings. My limbs. My candles.

get it all out, they say

You aren't coming next week. My calendar is filled less and less with red marker. Months go by. You are restless and moody. You want to move on. Your arm just there, near the edge of my chair. I could touch it if I tried. I could touch you, your crow-eyed face, and let you know how I cared and maybe let you take me on the bed like you used to, crawling over me, my legs spreading for you to smell and taste, for you to look up at me with hazy eyes, feel me tremble and quiver, kiss you long and hard, all tongues and wet, give this body something to dream about, to smell the sheets later, full of our come and lick them trying to retrieve you. I can't quite make my hand move over to you. Could you touch me? Could you tempt me to dance? Before signing out at the desk could you brush my hair or trace my neck with your lips just one last time?

Could you touch me?

Mycosis

The village, the one in the east, was threatened. Charlotte knew they were all threatened to a certain degree, but the east, due to its geography, was the most endangered. Naturally, it had become her most precious, the one she spent more time considering, the one that needed her most in order to flourish. There had been other problems over the last couple of weeks, problems that at the time seemed insurmountable, that had been conquered. And this too could be conquered if she put the correct plan into action and drew from all possible resources. She couldn't turn her back on them now. They needed her protection. Who else was there?

There were enemies. Some natural and some she hadn't counted on at the beginning of her mission. In fact, the whole thing had come as a surprise. The startling delicate treasure that she found in the corner of her bathroom against the light pink wall underneath the toilet, when she was on her hands and knees scrubbing the tiles after the shower pipes had burst. The plumber had left her late in the afternoon, after she spent three hours sitting, biting her blunt fingernails on the living-room sofa bed anticipating the heavy bill he would present her with. The bathroom floor was covered in mud from his work boots, streaks of brown and dotted black on the bathroom tiles pressed into the cracks. She had purchased the cream tiles not a summer ago, and couldn't stand a dirty bathroom. She got to work, filling the only pail she owned that came with a sale on sponges, a brighter pink than the walls, and began scrubbing the floor with hard and fast strokes as if it were a casserole dish. Then she saw it. Why hadn't she noticed before? Maybe it had just materialized, or maybe she had never looked hard enough behind the toilet. Perhaps it had been building over the last weeks or maybe months, sustained by the drizzle of shower water spraying over the metal curtain rod as the steady stream from the nozzle hit her arched back when she shampooed her long brown hair or bent over to soap up her legs for shaving. The toilet tank, right up against the wall and near the base of the bathtub, could have kept the area hidden from her view. Regardless, now she saw it. Growing.

At first she had been tempted to destroy the mushroom-shaped mould, its colour reminding her of the nicotine hue nails take on after decades of smoking. Her instinct was to put on her winter boots and jump on it to break its hold on the wall, or spray it with extra-strength disinfectant and watch it shrink by melting. She had already left to put on some thicker work gloves meant for gardening, not wanting to get her hands dirty, when something made her turn around and look again. She could have sworn the mould had changed positions, about a quarter of a centimetre from the white tiles, the mushroom's head titling upwards, like an open mouth. *Charlotte*, she said shaking her head as if to clear the thought from her mind, *nothing is out of the ordinary here. You're just upset about the pipes and the floor and the time it will take to finish with this mess. Keep to the original plan. Clean your bathroom. Put on a CD and drink a cup of tea.* But Charlotte didn't listen to her voice, *not that one.*

She dropped to her knees and edged towards the mould, her ear arched in the direction of its mouth.

The first thing she noticed was the smell, a piercing waft like earwax. As she managed to find a semi-comfortable position, resting the soles of her feet against the tub with her legs crossed underneath her and her left hand supporting the weight of her torso against the wall, the stench was instantly stronger, and brought a faint taste of bile to the back of her throat. Scrunching her nose, and cupping her hands over her mouth, she got used to it, the way she eventually got used to new weather when the seasons changed. The mould had shape, contours like a dome, and an indent on one side, thumb-sized. The colour of the indent was a mix of brownish-yellows and beige whites, a swirl close to an amber stone on her favourite necklace, and when she eventually let her fingers slide over it, poking to see if it was strong, it had the feel of thick rubber. She stood and backed up, taking in an aerial view. "My god," she exclaimed, "it's beautiful!"

Beautiful didn't cut it after a while. The Wet Lands, as she now thought of it, with its morphing shapes and hues like storm clouds, the way it forged its roots, the damp external layer slick as a raincoat, was miraculous. So was her conversion. Before she had been an obsessive cleaner and never allowed rust, lime, or mould to accumulate on any of her taps, hinges, or baseboards. Before moving into a new apartment, she hired cleaners, carpet steamers and exterminators. The most of the underworld she had ever witnessed had been ordinary dust. Sasha and her other friends continually complimented her on her cleanliness. Now mould prospered in her bathroom, underneath the same stone twin cat figurines on her toilet tank she'd bought because they resembled her cat, Oscar. This was not just ordinary mould, she was sure of it. This was like clay, formed from the inside out, in the constant act of becoming. She had to be a part of it.

After making herself some tea, the first thing she did was to rummage through the old shoeboxes stored in the upper shelf of her coat closet. It was there just as she remembered: the microscope, in its original package replete with Styrofoam packaging. She'd been given the instrument as a birthday present when she was admitted to college, not to study medicine, but her grandparents had meant well, they'd asked around for a good gift for a college girl and this is what they'd found. The only time she had ever used it (she'd dropped out of university after two semesters of accounting) was at her older sister's place. She brought the microscope over on several weekends free from her department-store clerk job, but her niece and nephew weren't very interested. They fumbled with the knobs and peered disappointedly through the lenses at their thumbs or spit, and then played with their other toys. After those few failed attempts, the microscope had sat in her closet, unused, and she hadn't even thought about it in years. Now she knew why she had kept it: it was time.

The specimen she extracted with her eyebrow tweezers took some fussing to get into focus. Charlotte was out of practice, the knobs, one adjusting the distance from the specimen, the other the thickness of the lens, moved awkwardly under her touch. The black plastic disoriented her eye with its shifting weight, light as an empty picnic basket. Then she glimpsed it. She readjusted the lens. Underneath her eye she counted ten long and narrow creatures like worms made out of thread, translucent and quick, skittering over the glass. She didn't want to lose any, reminding herself that they were real and not pictures out of a viewfinder or safely nestled behind glass at the natural history museum she had gone to with Sasha. She was anxious at the thought. How strange they were. They took no notice of her while she stood, bent over her kitchen table, her apron wrapped around her waist, marvelling at her discovery for hours, watching them move with the flexibility of acrobats, the dexterity of trained athletes. And yet, they were more marvellous, since they were born such. No need for training. They knew instinctively what their bodies were capable of, springing back and forth with dynamic energy, demanding her to be amazed. She unplugged the phone, put on some fresh clothes, and got started. *They will need things. They will need me.* She pulled a butter knife from her cutlery drawer, another pair of tweezers from her handbag, and a dried-out pen she had by the phone that she kept forgetting to throw out. She steadied herself, returning the specimen and its population back to the Wet Lands, and began to cut. First she made the thumb-print more defined, pushing it back to create a wider entrance. Next she pulled at the rubberish coating, cut a hole on the top of the dome, and filled it with fresh tap water. Finally she cleared the tile area of any other articles, banishing the toilet brush and garbage can to the kitchen. After that, her hands shaking with excitement, she made more tea, and then returned to refine the architecture of her village. The village. The Wet Lands. She did not anticipate others. One was certainly enough for anyone.

Two days later, running home from work, worried about her village, she was horrified to find her instincts had been correct. A large crater-like crack had appeared in the Wet Lands, as if someone had dropped a bomb. She collapsed to her knees, smacking them against the tiles and began to cry. *Why? Who? They aren't hurting anyone.* Then her keen eyes spotted the marks, five in total, nail prints.

She built borders by squeezing an upside-down laundry basket behind her toilet, and smacked Oscar on his nose. She hadn't thought about the cat. But she supposed they must be enemies now. There was competition for her affection. Too bad the cat was outnumbered, millions to one. But she also realized with a firm resolve that if she were to carry out the mission, not all of her creatures would remain unscathed or survive. There would be casualties and disasters. There would be explanations traded between them, rationalizations she would never hear, but life would continue and flourish. She watered her little Wet Lands and watched them grow. She would simply have to accept a death toll, and plod on.

A day later, since the only major problem with the Wet Lands for the moment was its location, dead-ended by the sink and the low wooden cabinet, which did not enable extensive westward growth, she opened her fridge to get some milk. She wasn't living on much more than tea and juice now, the excitement being what it was and her stomach being so delicate. She noticed the yogurt and then the sour cream. *The world works in mysterious ways*, she thought, and her new world was no different. Perhaps she had been plotting this new enterprise in the back of her mind, the first village a sign that others would eventually follow. The yogurt's expiry date was a week earlier, and the sour cream, hidden behind a bottle of unopened club soda she kept only for guests, was almost three weeks overdue. What had happened to her cleaning eye that she could miss it? The night before garbage day she always ceremoniously checked all the bottles and condiments in her fridge to make sure they were still fresh, a habit Sasha sometimes poked fun at. She hated mouldy cheese and bread especially. Maybe she hadn't noticed. Maybe she did and something kept her from trashing them. Either way, Charlotte was delighted with these distant relatives of her new world. She lifted the corner of a tub and caught a new smell, not like the Wet Lands, stronger, stingier, as if bad eggs had splattered all over the floor. She recoiled, dropping the lid on the floor, and splashed cold water on her face. Then she picked up the tub again. She thought she might actually throw up, putting her face so close to the sour cream that a tidbit of it smeared the tip of her nose, but she took deep breaths, held her ground and her nose to take a closer look. The greenish-blues were glorious mixed in the white; with a coat of fur she could touch, delicate as a spider's web, fuzzy like a beard. There were creatures in there, she was sure of it, and not trapped, but flourishing, expanding, moving. The microscope confirmed all her suspicions.

She collected the tubs on the ledge of her kitchen counter-top like plants, lids off, monitoring their growth, keeping them near light to aid the process along. The colours changed daily, suggesting their seasons ran on hourly cycles. She hadn't even anticipated having to defend them and herself until Sasha had come over to take her out for drinks. He hadn't discovered the Wet Lands, and why should he really, who bent over in your washroom to check behind the toilet? But he noticed the yogurt and sour cream on the window ledge, like congealed soap bubbles, and said "Jesus, Charlotte, have you seen this? You must have forgot to put these in the fridge. The smell … it's too much. Here." He grabbed a garbage bag from under the sink. Charlotte thought quickly. "Sasha — don't, I'm going to clean them. I just haven't had the chance yet. Such a waste of good containers." He shrugged and crumpled the garbage bag back into its drawer. Charlotte was proud of herself. In an instant, everything could have been over.

But that was a while ago, and the day and Sasha seemed very far away. He hadn't been over since, though he telephoned quite often. Everyone at work knew Charlotte was sick and would probably return in another week or so. Rumours circulated that she had pneumonia, or mono, or cancer. She told them she had a bad ear infection that caused vertigo. Why didn't anyone ever believe you told the truth about your health? Well, she had lied, but who wouldn't? Things were getting too close now. Only five days ago, her closest friend, Melinda, had stopped by with a pot full of chicken noodle soup. When Charlotte heard the knock at the door, she froze like a store mannequin and glanced at the Desert she'd started by the radiator, the heat sculpting tracks like dark brown sand. At night, in her sleep, she could smell the burning, a hazy smell like driving by a paper mill. The Desert was ruthless, constantly begging for her attention, mutating into mirages, the two bottom corners bulging like eternally open eyes. The knocking continued. She tiptoed out of her bedroom and locked the door, then draped a cloth over the Valley, a spontaneous night. Oscar scratched at her ankles.

"Charolotte? Charlotte? Are you okay? It's Melinda. I brought chicken noodle soup." *Oh Melinda*, Charlotte thought affectionately, relieved it wasn't Sasha who she didn't want to see right now — he walked into rooms without asking — or anyone from work. *I must let her in, but I can't let her know.* "Melinda? Just hold on, I need to put a housecoat." And she whipped off her cotton stretch pants that she'd worn two days in a row, chuckling to herself at how easy it was to put people on the wrong track, and wrapped the belt of her white robe around her waist. She shook down her brown hair, which had been tied into a tight bun to keep off her face as she worked, and rustled it with her hands. She sprinkled a bit of water on her forehead and pinched her cheeks. Then she opened the door with a half-hearted sickly smile.

The visit didn't last long. Charlotte feigned medicinal drowsiness. Although Melinda had obviously picked up on an offending odour, she kept it to herself. After Melinda left, Charlotte got back to work with her nail clippers and screwdrivers. The villages had taken on an air of progress: little squares like windows crafted into the fungi, pillars of flub and ooze carved into statues. Charlotte had built rivulets and walls, fortresses, and ducts with her tools. The Valley boasted bridges connecting one hill to the next, long stretchy fingers full of thick off-white goop. The Desert possessed an oasis she kept filled with tap water, its bottom smoothed into a gem-like rivulet. The Wet Lands, in the east, sprouted tall grassy fields. On the highest, she had even built a church. Three out of four rooms in her apartment (the living room reserved for her) were filled with stubborn life. She refused to use paint as the colours the villages blushed naturally were unreal — from mauve to orange, pinks, many shades of yellow, blue, black, dark with layers of happenings underneath the soil. She wondered how she had missed this all her life. Maybe she had simply forgotten the childlike thrill of digging in sandboxes and on beaches, sewer holes, and caves, where every child knew there were many intricate worlds thriving underneath the earth, propagated by the elements. Adulthood simply erased these discoveries, reopened only in fantasies and dreams, in the Technicolor late-night movies she sometimes watched when it was hard to sleep and she heard noises through the walls. *How privileged I am*, she thought. The next afternoon she got Melinda's answering machine and left a message. *The results are in, it seems I've got a mild virus, but it's contagious. I'll call when I'm allowed to see people again. Thanks for the soup. Love you.* It had not been difficult to mimic a mild virus. Charlotte had been coughing on and off regardless of her decision to wear a light cloth mask over her mouth when she went to investigate the Wet Lands or the Desert, and despite scrubbing her face with a terry washcloth after bending into the Valley's oily atmosphere. Then there was Sasha. *Of course I love you, yes I do, it's just that I'm contagious. No, I don't need you.* She wasn't sure she loved him though. He was far away, in another galaxy where they'd never have met if not for some strange collision. *We'll see each other soon.* He was determined that this was not healthy for their relationship, that after almost a year and a half of steady dating he should be involved in these things. There was nothing to be embarrassed about. *Oh, Sasha. Don't overreact. We'll survive.* But his voice quivered and it was evident he wasn't so sure about that.

Now that Charlotte had been off work for a few more days, well, another week, really, other problems had been dealt with fairly successfully. The bugs had been the most difficult, and the flies. She laid out traps in the different rooms, some boxed and others coiled, all lined with poison, and she also stood watch with spray, but it was hard to completely avoid contaminating her lands and she became very concerned about whether or not their atmosphere would be permanently affected. She remembered her high school lessons on evolution, that an aberration might occur but if it resulted in some kind of advantage the aberration would continue until it became natural and dominant. Progression of the species or something like that. It was all a blur. Theoretical. Here, all over her one-bedroom apartment in downtown Toronto, were real species, various kinds existing simultaneously with her, ones that might be harmed by her smallest movements, the chemicals she was spraying might fall like acid rain, marring their unseen faces, warping their invisible limbs. The thoughts of their demise weighed heavily on her conscience. She lived off water and canned goods, left from before when she kept her cupboards well stocked. She now only went out to get the mail. How were the bills going to get paid? She was out of sick-pay for the year. Maybe she would be thrown out, but if that was the case they would literally have to throw her out, kicking and fighting. Didn't she hear somewhere that possession was nine-tenths of the law? She would bar the doors and windows. She wasn't going to leave her world in the hands of strangers. She was everything to them. The only thing between them and disaster or annihilation. Their God, really.

Over the last two days the situation had grown out of control. The apartment, each room like a quarter of a compass, was beginning to stink. When she'd traipsed down the hall the day before, she'd hesitated momentarily at her own door, checking in case someone was watching. She had to put on her mask before re-entering. She even wore it to sleep. Her cough had grown chronic. The doors were kept shut. Oscar was left on the balcony. The Desert was boiling, as if its entire face had developed acne. Try as she might, flies swarmed around her, biting her gaunt arms and her exposed neck. The ants succeeded in burrowing, stealing pieces of her villages as food. She swatted at them, crushed them under her feet (these weren't her people) and even picked one's legs one by one. *An example for the rest*, she thought. For a while it seemed to make a difference. But the ants came back, like the cat in the old children's nursery rhyme she remembered. *The ants came back the very next day.* The pillars began to fall, the ducts drained of water. She wasn't sure which village was the worst off anymore. She tried forcing them out with loud music, but only extracted the anger of her neighbour pounding on her door.

The light was wrong, too. The light was warping the Valley. The original creatures she had discovered underneath her microscope had mutated. She loved them, regardless, but they were different. She filtered her water, cleansed her tools, spoke to them lovingly in calm tones she didn't feel. Still they were larger, a little hairier (Was that possible? Did they have hair?) but slower, easy prey. They had grown fat with prosperity. What could she do? She took a panoramic view, opening up all the inner doors of her apartment, and it was the east, the Wet Lands that were suffering the most. They were shrinking, decaying, and the wetness was drowning them.

The apartment had so many drawers and corners for

enemies to hide in and regain strength for another attack. And the food in the cupboards was dangerous. It attracted the enemy. If she had possessed the foresight, she lamented, she could have gotten rid of all her furniture, except for the bed and a chair, and marked off more substantial boundaries. But there was no time. For them to survive, they needed her. Charlotte knew this. The Valley overflowed from the windowsill down into the sink, vines extended to the ground. She no longer washed her own hands there or made her meals in the vicinity. Bits of mould were clogging up the drain. It was harder to walk carelessly around without clipping off a stalk — and how many beings were living on that stalk? How many? One day in anger, fighting with Sasha on the phone, she stomped unknowingly on a stretch of the Desert. She hung up and cried, knowing her creatures had no idea what was coming when the bottom of her slipper came down. Thousands, perhaps millions, dead. She couldn't stand it. Sasha had no idea the great things she was responsible for. Then there was the message she couldn't ignore: *Apartment 304 we have received complaints of a toxic smell ... coming tomorrow to check the floorboards ... may be dangerous, contagious ... want to inspect ... health standards.* A cold male voice. One she knew would not be sympathetic. Who would not bat an eye at killing her worlds.

After several hours of nail-biting, which she tried not to do since her nails were no longer clean, she formed a plan. She ran into the bathroom to tell her first land, now a planet, she thought, all planets with their own rules, about the idea. A glorious solution! As she left to check on the Desert and the Valley, she caught sight of her face in the mirror. She looked wild, her hair uncombed for days, plastered over her head like a smashed hat, and her eyes bright with red streaks, fine lines careening outwards. Her skin unusually tight, even for her. She moved her jaw up and down and it cracked. Still she was happy. She looked almost (almost) as if she had made love all night with Sasha and was heading to the bathroom to check her face, to see the joy she sometimes felt with the gentle throb of him still pulsing inside her. *I should have been nicer to him*, she thought. Then changed her mind. He was no longer necessary.

The spoon she held between her hands was silver, one of the gifts from her mother when she first moved into her own apartment. "You need things the first time on your own that you don't expect to need," her mother had told her. "You don't even think about them." This spoon was good for salads and soups when you had guests. Her mother was right, she hadn't thought much about entertaining. She had been thinking only of herself. But that was almost twelve years ago. She knew the lands could not survive on their own. They would need a different solar system, another galaxy in which to flourish. Charlotte was listening. She would answer their prayer. She began with the church in the hills and the fields on both sides, scooping them up and opening her mouth. *They need my protection. Who else is there?*

The Lilies

The thick cotton gardening gloves she had buried quickly, by the maple tree in the corner of the backyard, near the fence. The dog had shown too much interest in her quick digging, circling around her nervously, threatening to bark, and she had done a clumsy job. She would have to go back out and re-bury. The threat of the neighbours watching weighed upon her chest, or the thought of her husband finding her there, thinking she had gone crazy. He would blame it on menopause. He was not one to squirm at the word. Secretly, she believed, he enjoyed it. The hot flashes and fiery temperament, the need it created in her to be held. She had become a passionate woman again.

It wasn't the menopause, she knew, that caused the flowers. They were not visions she had created, though like most things in her household, she didn't understand their actions. Violet had lived amongst flowers before; they were her namesake. *How then,* she wondered, *can they just turn on you?* Drinking her rum and Coke, she sat slouched in the kitchen as the dishes stacked in the drying tub. She let the alcohol steep in her body. Maybe some sleep would help. But she was wide awake, and then there was Pickles, who was running around the hole, sniffing the evidence.

Priscila Uppal

Violet worked in a fruit-and-vegetable store part-time ever since her daughter Claire had moved away to Toronto. She had planted fruit and vegetable seeds for years, and her obsession had only grown with time. The way they smelled while roasting or boiling, how carefully you needed to separate the vines from entwining, and the stick of muddy soil between her thick-fingered hands to make them rise, all provoked her to keep growing. She planted every spring and reaped her harvest until the last days of autumn. Even chopping fruits and vegetables seemed a natural extension of her body. Firm rounded fingers eased themselves around knives and cutters, or the draining hole of a juicer. Working at the store helped her pass the time since her home no longer needed her full-time, not without Claire. Without Claire, there was no "little one" to bring up. "Bringing up Claire," she would gloat, "was my best work." Though it wasn't. The work was awkward and frightening in her hands as she watched the pig-tailed girl blossom into breasts and hips and thoughts about the world Violet could barely fathom. Not that Claire was what you could call "a bad seed." She wasn't. No angel, either. Inevitably, after a certain age, Violet knew a child no longer radiates innocence, but Violet had never found Claire innocent. Not even as a newborn. She had fallen from her womb, had tasted blood, and come out fighting for air. Her newborn, she feared, already had a bone to pick with a world that wouldn't contain her. Adult Claire now occupied an untouchable space, an area of tension like the one between her shoulder blades. Even the sound of her name out loud made Violet sense that Claire would eventually disappear from her completely like morning dew.

Sweat had doubly accumulated from the fear of the flowers and the rush of the alcohol, her face flush as if she had been baking all day. She sat envisioning her gloves underneath the ground rising like yeast into a white balloon with swollen fingers and wrists, digging their way back inside her house. Looking around the room, she tried to shake the thoughts off by repeating the names of common objects: dish, spoon, tablecloth, fridge. However, just as common as anything in her kitchen were the lilies outside. She tried not to think of their gramophone faces, the exposed seeds extended like insect antennae, or the sharpness of their leaves. *Stay still*, she told herself, as if the flowers were monitoring her movements, heads pointed like ears in her direction, afraid she might wake them from their resting. *Pour yourself some vodka.* But the alcohol made her blood warm, which sent her back to thoughts of blood. The blood bothered her most. The stench curled on the tip of her nose as she imagined a trail of blood from the gloves tunnelling through the backyard, feeding on itself, waiting to be discovered like oil. Or worse, it being autumn, they might be plotting to rise again in the spring. The dog, still sniffing the area with her hunter's nose, only confirmed her suspicions. She peed and Violet felt convicted.

The next morning she woke early. Stealing out of bed, as she did every weekday morning to make breakfast before Carl went to work, seemed sneaky instead of sweet today. She couldn't tell him about the violent flowers, and this morning she woke even earlier than usual, needing to confirm somehow by looking out her bedroom window that she hadn't imagined the whole incident. There they were: white lilies with their bonnets pulled tightly and tied under their chins, covered in dew as if praying.

She put on her runners and walked the length of scattered leaves to the store, grateful for the early opening of Mack's. She frequented Mack's at least two to three times a week. The small talk they had developed over the years charmed her. She knew nothing about his life, really; a few details: a wife, two children, one still at home (no idea what will become of him), the other a banker in Toronto. They were proud, decent. But who would know otherwise? Mack knew she liked poppyseed bagels in the mornings, a pack of cigarettes now and then for the evening that she asked for guiltily, like today, and that she had a sweet tooth for strawberry ice cream. He also knew her own daughter was somewhere amongst his family in Toronto.

"It's about time, isn't it?" Mack said, dropping the bagels into a brown paper bag in a swift natural motion.

Violet nearly choked on her words of greeting. Although Mack had been smiling when he asked his question, Violet was wary. Maybe someone had seen what happened yesterday in the garden. Maybe they were talking about her behind her back. She didn't know what time it was and was happy that she asked for cigarettes, had been shoving them into her robe pocket when Mack spoke. But he couldn't know about the lilies. No way.

"Time?" she asked. For breakfast? For the time of year she smoked more and, well, drank more? For Claire to return for a visit? She waited for his answer, searching past his inviting smile, reading off the brand names of cigarettes in her head.

"Time to freeze up the vegetables for the winter, eh, Violet?"

She handed Mack a ten-dollar bill, slightly embarrassed at not having caught on to his interest in her garden. He was a few years older than she was, but wore it well, his face relaxed into a soft circular jaw, his hair's lustre retained though it had lost its colour. Violet, however, thought she'd aged badly, liver spots stubbornly spreading across her arms and a good forty pounds over her hips and waist. She supposed Mack led a fairly ordinary life, same as she, but at the same time the money trans-action today felt like an admission of secretiveness. In fact, Violet wanted to take the money back after it left her fingers. She wanted it back inside her fist and wanted to run down the street in her terrycloth robe to her kitchen, fake being sick, and lie down on her sofa. *I'm going crazy*, she thought. *I always freeze my vegetables at this time of year. Everybody knows that on our street. What small talk could be more innocent?*

"Well, yes," she managed and then added, "another year." She smiled as she sighed, which made it seem as if she hadn't decided whether or not to be relieved or sad about the coming winter. Her garden closed every year at this time, reminding her neighbours of the overstock they would soon collect. Stashing the coins into the same pocket as the cigarettes, and turning to exit, the chime over the door sounded as another early-rising wife entered and headed straight to the cooler.

"Violet, you hurt your hand?"

Mack was holding the ten-dollar bill and turning it over. Violet looked down. Her hands were bleeding. Where the lilies had stabbed her, thin crusts of scab had opened, rose-coloured smudges across her fingers and palm as if she had squeezed a strawberry in her fist.

"Gardening?" Mack prodded as Violet studied her hands. "Can be a bit dangerous sometimes with all those tools."

"Yes." The other wife, with an armful of milk and eggs, was nudging her away toward the counter. Violet quickly offered her place and hurried home. Pickles was waiting to be let out. She let her out front.

Calling in sick for work was treated with friendly concern. Not feeling well? It's that time of year for the flu. Just had it last week. Drink lots of tea, rest up. *Time of year*, Violet thought, *for a lot of things*. The maple next door was already bare, the branches like old thin fingers that have lost the ability to grip. Maybe she was flirting with a flu. She had been sick with Claire twenty-seven years ago, this time of year. Pregnant, achy, and tired, Claire pushed her way around inside her belly, making room for arms and legs, a head that was too big for her small frame. Infant Claire, with her huge eyes and bald head, had reminded Violet of alien sketches she'd seen on television. Claire also watched her with an intensity that made Violet uncomfortable. *Just a little more Claire, eat a little more for Mommy.* Those words, Claire and Mommy, were strange to Violet. She liked telling her where to put the spoon better. Mouth. Hand to mouth. Shut. Swallow. And when she did, when she opened her mouth and took the spoon, Violet feared Claire would choke and she would be too paralyzed to save her, that she'd have to face a dead child in a high chair. When this didn't happen, Violet would burp Claire with vigour, wishing she could take some of the food back, that it might be too much, might try to break out of her stomach or through her feet. There wasn't enough room in her tiny body, not for all those mashed-up vegetables. Violet squeezed her violently in her worry, hoping Carl wouldn't blame her if the baby vomited. If the baby died.

Violet worried about many things and when the phone rang and she heard Claire's scratchy distant voice, she started to cry. *No dear, I'm fine, just the flu, not feeling well.* Even as adults, she mused, children rarely suspect their parents of faking sickness. She was glad. After a curt, "Too much gardening. I'm just exhausted is all," to explain her tears, Claire seemed satisfied.

"Can't come this year, Mom. Maybe in the new year. I'm working a lot and need the money."

Can't was a regular word in Claire's vocabulary.

"If you need money, dear, I can send —"

"No, Mom."

Can't, Mom.

Claire never accepted money from Violet unless it was

absolutely necessary. Violet had not yet seen Claire's apartment ("just wait 'til I get settled" was Claire's consistent reply
to that query), but thought she could certainly help out a little. Their mortgage was almost paid off now. She knew Claire
had roommates, one of them named Nikolai. Gay, apparently,
though Violet wondered whether Claire just told to her this
so she wouldn't pry about the living arrangements, or, more
importantly, the sleeping arrangements. Holding the phone
cord between her fingers, Violet curled it like hair. She couldn't
imagine the holidays without Claire. She heard a man's voice,
something about lunch, and Claire's characteristic hushing of
distractions.

"Is that a friend?" Violet couldn't help herself from asking.

"Sure, Mom." Claire chuckled a little.

Violet began to feel tears rising again. She never asked the
right questions to get a straight answer and wondered if her
daughter thought she was a joke.

"A boyfriend?" Oh, God, she knew that wasn't right. Claire
never called anyone a boyfriend. Violet felt constricted, her
breasts tight against her robe, which she hadn't yet discarded
for day clothes. They had never returned to their previously
small stature after Claire was born. Every few years, and even
now with menopause, her breasts have steadily continued to
swell. Perhaps due to her slow but steady weight gain, but last
month they even trickled a bit of milk. Nothing to bother the
doctor about, she had decided. Besides, from puberty onward
her body had never quite seemed her own. No one had ever told
her about the phases of menopause, though, the way they had
carefully laid out the stages of periods and pregnancy when she
was younger. She felt old, too old, talking to Dr. Affiffi about
every little worry and strange occurrence, about how she'd
begun to feel like a chemical factory that was breaking down.

The tears could be a symptom, too, she mused. *Maybe I need stronger pills.*

"Mom, don't get too excited. We just hang out. Nothing serious."

Violet nodded with familiarity. Every man in Claire's life was a nothing-serious. Violet was not deluding herself into believing that Claire didn't sleep with all the nothing-seriouses in her life. Claire would not marry a virgin. But neither had Violet, though it had been Carl who had first gained entry into her body. Carl was the only man to have seen her naked for almost fifteen years, before the affair and after — so short a duration it could not claim her imagination now even for a quick retreat. A failed attempt to kindle some excitement. She'd felt awkward with another man, as if he might be a foreign substance, a weed, perhaps. Sometimes she would come close to laughing hysterically as he tried to treat her like a young girl, telling her not to be nervous. No nervousness or worry had entered her mind in those few months. Not even the possibility of Carl finding out. He didn't, and she wasn't worried about wanting an affair ever again. She stopped seeing him when one afternoon he told her he loved her. After that, she didn't answer the phone. A few weeks and he stopped trying to get ahold of her in any way. It wasn't love he wanted to give her; it was space. So she grabbed her own, pulling her dress back on, folding up the couch, and walking home.

"Mom, I gotta go. Lunch."

I'm going. I gotta go. Claire said these words to her many times, and each time Violet felt as if clouds above the house were floating a little farther away, or darkening the way the days were shorter now.

"Okay, I love you."

"Me, too."

Violet believed her. Carl didn't any longer, and what she felt for Carl didn't stand up to the love she spoke for her daughter. Miles away, as closed off as she tried to make the lilies outside, she believed in Claire's love.

Violet had never planted flowers before. Although she knew her inexperience did not explain the actions of the lilies, she had never attempted to grow roses or pansies or a few tulips, not even to compliment her already blooming vegetable garden. When she had told Claire about planting flower seeds, Claire said it was her first garden. Violet had been offended. She liked to concentrate her energies on useful things. Flowers were merely decorations. She loved receiving them as gifts, imagined every woman did, like plaques to prove how well you've lived that people care enough to send them. But you couldn't eat a flower. Or at least she couldn't, although she had heard of using dandelion weeds to make tea and flower petals in sauces. But she didn't think you could cook them in all the ways she could cook her vegetables or eat them raw. You couldn't freeze a flower for later, retaining the original pungent flavour. You couldn't chop and boil flowers with the same exactness or scent, hold them in your hands and rip them open, biting hard like into an onion with its sting in your eyes. Chopping an onion and crying when you've grown it yourself is an accomplishment. Onions are also a wonderful device when you need to cry and don't want to explain your tears. You can count the rings of an onion the way you can those of a fallen tree. Flowers have no such double natures. And carrots, their long bodies thrusting through the soil, slipping into her hands like an umbilical cord. Carrots go with any meal. Carrots add colour, like flowers, but they are also practical and useful. Good for the eyes. No old wives' tale. Violet boasted twenty-twenty vision. No matter how hard she tried to avoid the view of her dozen lilies from the screen door, she couldn't, and her hands had started to bleed again, trickling red droplets over her large breasts.

"What happened?" Carl asked as Violet dished out mashed potatoes and sweet peas.

He had been home for almost two hours, watching the evening news and then talking on the phone to his brother in Halifax. Violet had always been hurt that she'd been an only child, and considering her longing for other siblings to play with and talk to, Carl hadn't understood when Violet insisted she didn't think she could handle having another child. Money had been tight then, before Carl's promotion. Violet argued their finances couldn't support another, and Claire had been such a handful as a toddler that they dropped the subject for a couple of years. Couldn't handle. Not didn't want. But that's really how Violet had felt. She didn't want any more children. Playing games with Claire, she found herself inadequate, without the right imagination, and Claire would grow agitated. *Of course cows can fly to the moon, Mommy. No, Claire, they can't, they are animals. They can't even think.* Claire would throw her toys across the room. Plastic figurines returned to her play chest with scuffed paint or missing limbs. Violet would dump them all together, knowing Claire had not meant to harm her little toys in anger. It was Violet she wanted to send across the room so she didn't have to play with her anymore. Violet was relieved when Claire took to the mysteries of books, places she didn't have to invite Violet to enter, lands where animals thought and visited the moon.

Claire looked a lot now as Violet had then. Pretty, though not the soft stunning features of some girls that make them appear fragile. They were strong women, what men once called "child-bearing girls." Fertile, strong-lined, smooth-featured, but not enough to be distracting. Sturdy, like crocuses.

"I cut them gardening. It's nothing to be worried about, just a couple of scratches."

Violet's answer seemed to satisfy Carl. Steve, his brother, has a new girlfriend, he told her.

"Do we still call them girlfriends at that age?" Violet asked jokingly.

They glanced up from their plates at each other with the secure look of a couple justified by the unstable relationships around them. It was a pleasant moment for Violet and she poured herself some more wine.

"Did Claire call?"

"Mondays like clockwork with her. I wonder when she'll have a boyfriend. A real one, you know? Is Steve's woman nice?"

"Any woman's nice if you haven't met her yet."

She laughed, napkin over her lips in case any potato might fall out.

"Don't worry about Claire. She was a late bloomer. She'll phone to tell us she's getting married soon enough."

Violet put her fork down. "But we never hear about —"

"Maybe if you didn't pester her about it all the time ..."

They'd re-enacted this conversation countless times since Claire had moved. At this point, Violet wondered whether she even wanted Claire to get married. Claire always had her own way, especially as a child. Violet found it difficult to discipline her when she didn't understand her actions. Maybe Claire's attitude towards boyfriends and marriage was another space Violet would never be able to enter. Men and marriage might not interest Claire in the least. What are you doing? Violet would ask her. *Taking a few courses, you know, working. I'm in a samba class on Saturdays.* These were typical responses. But what are you doing with your life? The silence at the other end of the line made her fearful that Claire wondered the same about hers.

"More wine?" Carl was pouring the last of it already into his own glass, pushing away his chair to pile the dishes. Violet ate slowly. When you grow your own food, she told him, and you have to wait so long for it to be ripe, it takes a little longer to stomach. To consume it too fast is an insult. Besides, tonight she was already tipsy from sneaking drinks all afternoon, even letting Pickles sniff her glass to see if she wanted to join her. Her appetite was shrinking.

Later, when she washed the dishes, she couldn't help seeing the lilies, marked off by the twine used to enclose the vegetable garden. Their full area couldn't be more than six or seven feet, and yet they seemed to be taking up more and more room. Perhaps it was the shadow created by the porch light that made the lilies stand out, but they obscured the vegetables, continuing to grow at an astonishing rate. Stretching out thin necks, glaring at her. A rising jury.

She soaked her hands in the hot water until they felt disembodied and useless. She always felt a little like this after Carl talked to his brother. Like an outsider, even if she could amuse herself with the idea of a middle-aged man having a new girlfriend. Carl and his brother weren't that close, but they updated each other on the important things. Violet envied them since her conversations with Claire would never be on the same par as siblings. Someone would always be judging the other from a level up or down.

Carl was a man of routine. Watching television again, he would soon take his nightly walk with the dog. *Nightly walks keep old couples together*, Violet frequently thought. You can imagine they're leaving. Never coming home. Every evening that possibility existed, that chance, and when they return home you are pleased, but wonder why? Why didn't they just turn right again, or left, or get on a bus, hail a cab, run or crawl away from the houses they will most likely die inside? Why, for that matter, did the dog stay? She supposed guaranteed shelter and food were the answers. Maybe people weren't that different.

Violet took the opportunity to enter the garden, thinking her day of rest might have made her stronger somehow to face the lilies. She'd chosen the lilies from a new selection of plants in the store. Supermarkets were selling too much produce so the manager decided people still don't trust their flowers to large companies. They prefer a local feel. Steadily, the store introduced flowers and plants, seeds and new gardening tools. Mostly varieties easy to care for, that don't need a great deal of attention or particular soil, so each customer would soon have a colourful windowsill to greet them in the morning. When she asked Carl if he had an opinion on lilies, he informed her Florence was sometimes called the City of Lilies. A girl named Lily in high school told him that. She didn't choose the lilies because of Florence. Violet had never been there. She chose lilies for their wide leaves, and white lilies because gardening for months in the dirt and mud sometimes made her feel dirty. Lilies could give the garden an air of purity or graciousness. But her lilies proved otherwise.

In the evening they had shrunk in size, leaves tucking into themselves the way cats do when they don't wish to be disturbed. She thought of nuns in their habits, how whenever you thought of nuns they were never moving, always quiet and still. These lilies too seemed to know something unseen. Violet also knew strange occurrences frequently arose in autumn as stalks decayed and last chances for seeds to sprout were grabbed. Tomatoes pushing up black, onions with skin tight as rubber. But she had never seen flowers inch closer together, as these lilies did, as if for warmth. And their roots were twisted, like broken limbs, holding on, refusing to die their deaths like the other plants, refusing to give up. Maybe that's why they were so angry. Perhaps they thought she controlled the weather.

Or maybe it was as simple as water. No rain for a couple of days. And Violet would welcome rain, so she didn't have to water the lilies herself, and so the blood from her gloves might mix with the rain and chase away the scent of them. She might even wash her hands in that rain. An autumn rain felt as if hibernation was nearby, a few sheltered months. Soon she would collect all her vegetables and load excess off to neighbours: tomatoes, cucumbers, peppers, zucchini, peas, and carrots, until they would be wary of her arms dishing out more vegetables. She and Carl would eat from her garden every night for months as if tricking winter.

You couldn't save flowers that way. Another reason Violet had found flowers impractical. How depressing to watch them wilt, struggling upward as leaves turned arthritic, until the flowers matched the stem and became a long hard stick, like a dead body to bury. What guilt, especially with annuals. *At least lilies are perennials*, she rationalized when she bought them. Now the promise of another season seemed like a threat.

Also, flowers never apologize. Not the way vegetables do by making the ground more fertile for next season. In fact, she had watched many flower-growers despair over their gardens that looked worse each year if not for continuous strategized replanting. The first bloom the most beautiful; other seasons were failed attempts to recapture initial glory. Violet knew flowers were a bad idea, but she couldn't help herself. She wanted them. Another pair of cotton gardening gloves on her hands, she began on her knees, crawling with her elbows far enough away from the lilies to retreat if she needed to. She felt silly, but it was already dusk and if the neighbours were watching over the fence or through their windows they couldn't clearly see what she was doing. One of her gardener's tricks, perhaps. Coaxing cucumbers to fill out or protecting tomatoes from bruising. More than silliness, she felt dangerous on the soil inside the wooden stakes with the fine chicken wire as if she were on display or had crossed the fence of someone else's yard to steal a garden gnome, lure the neighbour's kitten to her porch for milk.

The lilies seemed to waken or maybe it was the breeze, but Violet's heart started pumping quicker. There was a stiffness to them, an alertness. She stopped in her tracks, and though she hadn't been out long, she was wary Carl might return soon, forgetting the custom Colts cigar he allowed himself on his evening strolls. To turn back into the house and pretend a headache, draw a warm bath, was a better idea than being a middle-aged woman confronting hostile lilies. She started to speak softly to them, words unwound from a deep knot in her stomach: *I won't hurt you. I don't want to hurt you. I just want to touch. I want to make sure.* With each phrase she inched forward, hand first, since her hands were protected. Slowly, then quickly, since the lilies were oblivious to her, she progressed, and Violet began to believe she really had dreamed up the whole violent incident of the night before. Then, finally in front of the lilies, she allowed her gloved hands to stroke the stalks, the long green leaves, with a tenderness that surprised her. Feeling the urge to laugh, to kiss the white heads resting close to her chin, she forgot about protection. Her guard down, the nearest lily turned and slapped a white petal across her face.

"I don't feel well, Carl." Hand mirror held against her face, Violet would not let him in. "Use the one downstairs. I don't want to come out yet." Without answering her, she could hear his steps down the stairs and soon after the flush of the toilet and his return.

"Don't stay too long or you'll prune. Good night, honey."

"Good night. I'll be there soon." *And he'll be asleep,* she thought. *How will I sleep, knowing what the lilies think of me?* The bruise wasn't dark enough for anyone to notice, she convinced herself. And it wasn't. She just looked flushed, a schoolgirl on a first date who'd spilled a drink on her dress, nervous by the possibility of rejection. No possibility here. Plain, utter rejection. And she was no schoolgirl, her face in the mirror reminded her. *But they let me touch, a little, just a little.* She soaked in the hot water, her breasts hovering halfway inside and out. Her nipples too had changed size over the years, larger, but flatter, a purplish tinge with fine creases from the stretching. Sometimes she thought they had minds of their own. Maybe they were tired of sticking out on top and were steadily spreading themselves in order to fold back inside of her. Hands unbandaged, she let the left sway over them until the heat relaxed her. Moving her hips, the swoosh of tub water excited her. She let her hand fall farther until she was flushed from herself. Almost content, she dried herself and opened the door only to find Pickles wagging her tail, the bloody gloves held firmly in her mouth.

Two days sick from work was actually more justifiable than one. It meant you really needed to recuperate from whatever bug had grabbed you. Not the lazy bug, which could be suspected after only one day off. She assured her co-workers she'd be back to normal by the end of the weekend, in time for her next shift. But Violet was not convinced. She'd spent three hours down in the basement with bleach and cleaner and a metal tub, scrubbing the gloves with a fierceness she rarely felt anymore. The dog didn't want to let go, and she had to place her hands at the crook of her mouth and separate the jaws the way the vet had taught her to administer medicine when she was ill. Once the gloves were clean and more than a little torn by her obsessive pulling, she dropped them in the trash can next door — she couldn't bear to put them in her own — happy that garbage pickup was in the morning, and refused to let Pickles out until the truck arrived at 5:00 a.m. It bothered Violet that the dog knew her blood. The hole outside had also bothered her and she didn't wait until morning to refill it. She scooped dirt the size of anthills back in the hold, patting the soil until the surface looked natural. At the corner of her eye, she thought she'd seen the lilies smile, their white mouths slightly curled on the sides. She went to bed, too exhausted to take a shower, her fingernails and the back of her hands slicked with dirt. Carl didn't notice.

Once Carl left for work, she sped to the local library. Was it something she had done wrong: soil, water, placement, fertilizer? Recognizing the librarian at the checkout as one of her regular customers, she quickly picked five books off the shelf, explained she was in a hurry, and returned home. Pickles was jumping up and down in front of the back kitchen window, barking. She could not be distracted until Violet lured her into the living room with treats. Then they both lay down on the couch and slept.

The books weren't much help. Lilies of the Valley. A common variety of garden plant. *Convallaria majalis*, whatever that meant, though it sounded nice spoken aloud. One book claimed her breed of flower displayed "two long oval leaves and spikes of white bell-shaped flowers."' The language startled her. Spikes were dangerous. Wasn't this an ordinary flower, which she had thought meant purity and innocence? When did it develop blades for hands? *It could be worse*, she told herself as she kept reading. She could have chosen tiger lilies, or Turk's cap lilies.

She discarded the books, deciding none could possibly mention what she was searching for, and spent the afternoon in front of the television, a rarity. She usually only watched with Carl. Today, however, the snippets of soap operas commandeered her for hours. She even made popcorn, thankful Carl wouldn't be able to smell it by the time he got home, feeding some to the old girl, who couldn't be blamed for digging up suspicious objects in her territory. Isn't that the original reason they had bought Pickles, for protection? Though she barely barked anymore, this morning's exhibition a rarity, as well, Violet forgave her now that the gloves were safely in a garbage truck out of town. She didn't tell Carl she'd stayed home the last two days. Didn't need to. He hardly ever went to the store, so there was no chance she'd be caught playing hooky. Never the type as a kid, too afraid to risk it. But Claire did, and when she was caught and Violet would scold her about wasting her day, Claire would glare back at her, confounded. "I was exploring," she'd say. Claire always found new places to explore, such as Toronto.

Even the wrecked lives of the soap opera characters couldn't keep Violet from thinking about those lilies barred by two closed doors and one screen. When the phone rang she thought for a second the lilies were screaming.

"Mom?"

"Yes, honey, hello. Sorry, you startled me."

"Just me, Mom."

Her second rum and Coke of the day was trickling down her bathrobe. *Becoming a bit of a lush*, she had thought pouring it, and was somewhat pleased she could develop an awful habit later in life. As her aunts and uncles had grown older, they all seemed to drink and smoke more and maybe this was just the way it happened: afraid to go outside, content in a bathrobe in front of the television with a stiff drink, or two, or three.

"You didn't sound so good yesterday so ..." Claire sounded apologetic as if phoning her mother too often was embarrassing.

"No, thank you." She poured herself another drink. "I'm feeling better."

"That's good, Mom. I just wanted to check."

Checking up on me? Violet mused. *Like the lilies. Making sure I'm in line.* But Violet didn't want Claire to go. Frantic for something to say, she blurted, "I still sleep with your father, you know. Not the way we used to of course, but he still performs and I still want it now and then. He's a good man."

"Mom!"

"No, really," Violet added defensively, turning off the television to hear herself speak. "I still have orgasms. Sometimes I make them happen myself. But I'm not dead yet." Her hand, which had given her pleasure the night before, pushed slightly against her thighs.

"Mom." Claire's voice was softer now. "Mom, are you okay? Are you taking your medication?"

"Yes!" Violet cried. "But I can still love, Claire! I love you, honey."

Violet was drunk with herself. She wanted to kick all the tiny figurines on the mantle — ones she had collected over the years and only noticed when dusting — down with her toes. She wanted another drink. She wanted to hug Claire so hard it would hurt her. She began to hum.

"Mom, I'm going to come home, after all, just a little later, and here —"

"That's wonderful. I'll tell your father. I have to go now."

"But —"

"Don't worry." Violet swallowed the rest of her tumbler,

inebriated too by the fact that Claire would be with them for the holidays. "I'm fine. Call me soon. I love you."

"I, ah, Mom, I love you, too. Are you sure?"

"Yes. Goodbye."

Violet wasn't sure, so she checked. Yes, she had taken her medication: Provera and Premarin. The menopause combination with names as pretty as flowers. A tiny blue pill and a slightly larger red oval one regulated her hormones. She had thought the red pill should have been made pink, like baby colours before a child's sex is known and you buy pink and blue everything. And now her body had no idea what sex it was. Violet feared she was becoming neutral, but took the pills anyway. Many women were on these pills, her doctor assured her, and suffer very few side effects. *Did they all have violent flowers?* she joked to herself. *I should ask him that one.*

Going over her conversation with Claire from the afternoon in her head, she now felt embarrassed. Claire will laugh about it with her friends later, she imagined, how her mother tried to convince her she was sexy. But maybe they would admire her a little for her honesty, hoping they too will want to get into the sack after they raise their own children. Making stew for dinner, throwing a combination of spices into the pot as well as a few of each vegetable she had confidently grown, Violet thought, *I should've told her I was stranger when I was younger.* In case Claire decided she had suddenly become absurd. Giving birth to Claire, she was at the height of her strangeness, as if she were floating in space and someone had handed her a baby like getting a life jacket thrown at you in a dream when you believe you might be drowning. *And braver, too. I think I was much braver.*

After dinner, Violet sneaked out again. That's the word she

heard inside her head as she shut the screen door. Sneaking into the evening. She knew now that the lilies would probably let her touch them again, but no gloves. Bandages were discarded in the garbage underneath the kitchen sink. She could already see their bodies stretching, their white enigmatic faces. And if they turned on her tonight, she knew she wouldn't walk away this time. She would wrestle with them until they came up breathing from the other's grip. Unbuttoning the top of her blouse, she slid down to her knees, and began to ground herself with words: soil, stem, blossom, petal, child. It had started drizzling a half an hour earlier and Violet realized she might have to explain to Carl if she came in soaking wet, but she didn't care. He would have to let it go. It was time to face the lilies on equal ground.

The Man Who Loved Cats

"The whole of her feline face was striving towards a universal language, towards a word forgotten by men." — Colette

The Man Who Loved Cats had three beautiful daughters, each one lovelier than the next in his imagination, who lived in three different cities and sent letters and postcards dated meticulously and economically in tiny white envelopes. He would slice open the letters while lounging in his reading chair situated beside three arm's-length scratching posts and a bed of fresh catnip. The cats purred loquaciously, butting their foreheads into the catnip and against the chair legs as he read, no matter what news was afoot. He read out loud, and sometimes one of the cats, the tabby orange-tailed short-hair named Tug in particular, would jump into his lap and press his paws like rubber stamps against the papers. On Tuesday the fifteenth of June, he told Tug and the others: My daughters are coming to visit me. It seems I am going to die. Tug batted the length of the paper and the nine cat noses surreptitiously buried in the catnip forged a wedge. A ball of twine beside the hole sat stationary as a stone.

The Man Who Loved Cats also loved black-and-white films and the Book of Revelations. He loved asparagus and potatoes, soup cans in military order on their shelves, homemade short-bread with lots of white sugar, and orange pekoe tea. He loved a crisp autumn wind and daffodils, the sunflowers on the lawn at 282 Robert Street, the way the curbs dropped to accommodate his shopping cart. He made his way down to the twenty-four-hour store every weekday morning at 8:00 a.m. and was served by a middle-aged cashier named Yolanda. He told her that his daughters were coming to visit and she congratulated him. He told her he was thrilled. She said she was thrilled for him and double-bagged his items and punched in an extra thirty-cent coupon for his milk from the flyer. It's because I'm dying, he told her. Yolanda said nothing. He paid her by cheque and she validated it. The Man Who Loved Cats was ninety years old before he began to think of the future.

On Wednesday the thirtieth of June, the three daughters arrived on separate trains from three different cities. They arrived by age at the hour; the oldest at one, the middle child at two, and the youngest at three. He spent two days cleaning his bungalow, arranging cat toys into plastic bins, placing dishes of food and water in clusters, dumping out litter, brushing and bathing each of his cats, even the ones afraid of the deep claw-foot bathtub, and inserting nametags into every collar. There was the long-haired Persian, Lorca; the four black-and-white tuxedo kittens, Kato, Kiko, Stoney, and Winston; the calico cats, Hamlet and Ophelia; a seal-point Siamese, Ike; the tortoiseshell couple, Thyme and Basil; the chinchilla with stomach worms, Socrates; the Burmese with the limp leg, Tatiana; and Lucy, Dixie, Junior, Professor, Moses, Nero, Zoltan, Zeus, Whiskers, Jazz, Jive, Casey, Max, Molly, Bubbles, Tinker, Vergil, and Ovid. They received two chewy dental treats at the end of the session. The few stragglers hiding under beds and in empty cardboard appliance boxes were left out, as well as the old short-haired Pepper who had been gallivanting outdoors for three days now. But all in all they were prepared to meet the beautiful daughters of their master.

When each of the three daughters arrived, she kissed her father on the forehead and put down her luggage. Each smiled at the furry congregation without picking any of them up. The oldest wiped her chair before sitting down and when The Man Who Loved Cats made orange pekoe tea, the youngest picked a long marmalade hair out of her saucer. The middle daughter took it upon herself to serve, opening the wrong cupboards, startled by the amount of dry cat food bags, wet food cans, treat tins, lactose-free milk cartons, sachets of catnip, and a pharmaceutical array of liquid medicines and pills to fight fleas and ringworm, cat acne, and eye infections. She finally found a tin of sugar biscuits with Christmas ribbon still taped to its cover and placed them in the middle of the kitchen table for dipping. What do you eat? she asked her father. You have grown so thin.

A few of the bravest cats manoeuvered between their legs while some slept obliviously and some, like Junior, the cream long-haired cat with the black dot under his chin, kept a considerable distance and stared at the beautiful interlopers. Their father said, It seems I am going to die. The oldest took his hand and said No. The middle daughter shook her head while the youngest continued to sip her orange pekoe tea. Yes, he said, yes, I am going to die and it is time to think about the future. He had tears in his eyes as he scanned his daughters, the oldest a dark-brown short-haired slim beauty, the middle an ash-blond long-haired tall debutante with shiny red nails, the youngest the shortest one with raspberry shoulder-length hair and pin-striped ginger streaks. How could he choose between them? he silently asked Basil at his feet. How to choose which one?

The daughters told their father they didn't want to talk about his death, but he insisted. I must put things in order, he claimed, and prepare to distribute what I own. The oldest daughter finally retreated, As you will Father, and they left the kitchen for the living room where The Man Who Loved Cats placed the extra milk from the tea into small plastic dishes as a means to get the cats off the couch and lounge chairs. It took a few minutes for the mewing and synchronistic lapping to subside so that he could begin properly again. Before he did, Pepper sauntered in through the cat door and plopped himself at his master's feet, a tuft of fur missing from his right ear, his bright eyes on guard against the three beautiful daughters. I must know how much you love me, he said. And immediately the oldest and the middle daughters spoke in unison: We love you to the depth and breadth of our souls. We love you as the sun loves the earth in summer. We love you more than the faithful love God. We love you the way no daughters have ever loved their fathers. We love. Love.

Then they broke off, the oldest saying, I have a husband and two children who also love you, though I couldn't bring them on this visit. The middle daughter said, I have loved you too much to marry or have children to replace you. I suppose you must think of the grandchildren, said the oldest. Think of the children you have, said the middle daughter. The Man Who Loved Cats felt an old happiness thinking of the love of his two daughters and when they were young and would come in from playing and sit on his lap, or when they would be tucked into bed or spoon-fed pudding from his hands. He hadn't much money then, and they loved him when he trundled in from work tired and achy and stretched thin to the bone. They loved him, he told himself. It is certainly true. And Lorca bounded across the carpet in sympathetic joy.

But you have said nothing, he said to the youngest daughter

with the shimmering fur. How much do you love your father? And the youngest daughter continued to stay silent as her sisters anxiously awaited a response. Their father rose from his seat and approached her. Stand up, he said, look me in the eyes and tell me how much you love me. I am dying. The youngest rose from her place, shaking underneath her blue wool sweater, her hands gripping the frame of her chair. She pushed a loose strand of hair off her forehead and obeyed. I love you as much as I have to, she said. Same as mother did. He could not believe what he heard, or that none of the cats attacked her for her insolence, or that the other two sisters were equally silent in their chairs. He lifted an arm and was ready to swipe at her clean and polished face to leave his mark. Instead, he was stopped by the resemblance of this girl to her, his dead wife, the one he loved more than them all. He ran out the door, Hamlet and Ophelia at his heels until the end of his street.

Although it wasn't a Friday night, his usual schedule, he entered Mayday Malone's and sat at the bar, ordering a draft beer. Marshall, who always had his mug filled and ready by 8:00 p.m. on Fridays and made the same crude joke about the number of women he must be seeing by all the different colours of hair strewn across his clothes, at the sight of his sad and distracted face told him that this one was On the Bar. He ordered a club sandwich and fries and dipped each fry into the gravy, shaking his head mournfully. I'm dying, he told Marshall, and ordered a second beer. Marshall obliged. My daughters are visiting and I love them, you know. Mashall did know, said we all love our kids no matter what. True enough, he replied, his head bent towards the solitary pickle on his plate. But what if they don't love you? he silently asked his fork.

For two days he got up and went to the grocery store and traded pleasantries with Yolanda and spent his afternoons at

Mayday Malone's. He bought a ticket at the discount movie theatre on Bloor Street since they were showing *The Maltese Falcon*,
one of this favourite black-and-white films, and read Revelations
at night. The cats tried to comfort him, sleeping curled in perfectly precious shells, purring against his chest, running across
the floors as if nothing was out of the ordinary, fussing over
him in the evenings when he finally came home. He refused to
open his bedroom door and the three beautiful daughters tried
to entice him to come out. I'm dying, he told them. Don't you
understand? And his chest did feel heavy underneath the tuxedo
kittens perched upon him, and he began to cough and cough
and cough.

On the third day he awoke to his regular purrs and meows
without the heavy-footed creaks on the floor or swoosh of the
tap water. He found the letter on his grocery cart as he was leaving. It said: We are sorry for our sister's ingratitude and that it
has made you unhappy to be with us. We will come to visit you
again before you die. We love you. The youngest daughter did
not leave a letter in a tiny white envelope, but she left a short note
on a napkin attached to a bottle of syrup on the counter. Try this
Father, it might help. Yours. Then her name.

Instead of going to the store to talk to Yolanda, who kept
asking him to bring in his beautiful daughters sometime to help
him carry his groceries, The Man Who Loved Cats remained
home in his reading chair, the letter on his lap and the napkin
in his pocket closest to his heart. He thought of his wife and
how she could never sleep soundly, always tossing and turning, getting up and pacing in the middle of the night, and how
when he came home from work distressed and dirty her eyes
would widen the way those of the cats did when he dropped
things clumsily on the floor. I am dying, he told his cats, the
variety of colours like the wreaths he knew would soon encircle

him, and Zoltan licked his rough tongue across his sweaty arm. When he coughed again he jumped. Then, almost as if written in careful, delicate handwriting, he recalled a passage he had read in one his books, long ago, when he was first deciding after his wife's death and the daughters' disappearances whether or not he wanted cats: As with everything a cat does, it is not always easy to distinguish between the innocently curious or deviously clever methods of attracting attention. He ate his cream of asparagus soup and went to sleep amongst his kind.

The Man Who Loved Cats died in his own bed, in his own home, on Sunday night, July fourth. The pound took his cats away, rounding them up like scattered leaves, separating mother from child, brother from sister, friends from lovers. In the end, he could not decide who to leave his cats to, but his beautiful daughters inherited all the money, as the will had stated since his wife died. And his daughters came to the funeral, opened black umbrellas and left, and in three different cities, they care for dogs.

The Still Body Is the Perfect Body

Though Drucilla knows it isn't quite like that. Her body is still, her armpits in half-moons aching to collapse onto themselves, a wedge of skin pinched between the chair and her thigh, her hands upon her lap. Only perfect in that she is naked and the students will attempt to draw her to scale. Sometimes she likes to stay after class, once her terrycloth robe is safely around her shoulders. Some students leave quickly, but others stick around to talk and trade glances at drawings. Occasionally, she asks to see some of the sketches, usually glad that they miss little features that irritate her. That they don't catch the strawberry birthmark on the side of her knee, which makes her lovers think they've given her an odd love-bite, or the thin wisps of light-brown hair around her belly button. She shaves carefully each morning in order to ensure a perfect triangle between her legs. Geometry is important.

Lines are essential. Lines to keep her on the paper, tidy and neat at the centre of a page. Lines to contain the inside of the body. Points to connect parts of the body, building a universe out of disjointed shapes. At times she imagines her portrait coming alive under their busy pencils scratching the surface, the only noise in the quiet, except for the ignored tiny shifts she steals for herself in fear of becoming completely numb. When a foot is asleep it's actually a blessing. Stillness is no longer a choice. Imagining that portrait spilling over the pages, drool falling from her lips soaking the corners of sketchbooks, hair growing like thick spiderwebs, blood trickling down her legs onto their thighs. The laps of the younger ones are hard and crossed because the naked body is still a novelty, like driving a car for the first time. A privilege, but felt to be a right.

Her hip is itchy. Holding in her breath, she slides down minimally in the chair to rub bone against wood. They don't pay fifteen dollars an hour to change angles in mid-session. Even the teacher is using her for a model today. He says he likes to now and then to remember the discipline of his art. Sometimes he's hard on the students. They think they are born artists and look baffled when he insists that repetition in the service of craftsmanship is the goal for the year.

Drucilla wonders about the teacher, his brown corduroy blazer out of place in the studio. Is he married? She has never bothered to check for a ring, but she can't help but think his wife picks out his clothes. He is clean-shaven, yet his eyebrows are thick and fall out of line with the rest of his round face. She wonders if he's ever asked his wife to pose, knowing her body in his hands, but not necessarily in the bright light of a studio to be critical of its shapes and contours. Woman. Not wife. Or the back he perhaps adores for the way each vertebra longs to be read by his fingers, and now thinks *ladder*. Draw spine like a ladder or the creased backing of a book, a covering for what he really reaches to inside when he takes his clothes off and enters her in the privacy of a dimly lit and familiar bedroom.

Careful, she thinks, taking quick note of her own pink nipples, slightly erect, although they are conscientious here and keep the temperature warm in the life-drawing studios. Let the mind wander too much and the body is less obedient. It isn't paying attention to itself.

She stares at the white-painted wooden platform she is raised upon, half a foot from the ground (not a real half-foot, she thinks), and recalls the time the teacher, after class, found her at a campus bus stop on a wet November afternoon searching for change in her disorganized purse. He gave her a ride, letting her off at an intersection close to her home. Although he didn't hire her personally, and had probably never thought much of her body except as an art object, she felt shyly uncomfortable beside him in the car, while he asked her questions she answered by rote, how she likes the area she lives in and when she hopes to graduate from university. She couldn't stop herself from speculating that since the space between herself and his desk had shrunk that he must be wondering what her body actually felt like. Not as listed on the form: thirty-eight, thirty, thirty-six, long straight brown hair, medium-boned, medium-beige skin; but how these dimensions and qualities would move, hair on chest or hips circulating pelvis, whether her skin was dry or oily, if she would ebb in a rhythm similar to his own. Would he compare her to other models he had seen? Or to women he had known when he was younger, not middle-aged and balding around the crown, when he didn't require ulcer pills and he could drop his pants with confidence?

At times Drucilla thinks her eyes soak in the light from the window and fluorescent bulbs over her head as she spreads it out to the students in the form of a still-dance. Like the sun. It appears most of the time that the sun is moving, but really it is us in endless orbit around that light. She senses the students' gazes and their charcoal pencils orbit her body elliptically, extracting what they need, absorbing her as a still emission of energy to transform into flat substance.

Checking the clock, she notes that the session is half over. She only has to keep her pose for another fifteen minutes. It is always the first and last few minutes that are the most straining. The first spent settling into the proper position for the sitting or standing, worrying if her muscles are up to the challenge today, if they will cramp up or ache like dull weights, if she can present herself with some elegance. The last minutes her body speaks to her in various ways: a push on her belly asking to use the washroom, her toes curling upwards the way a flower turns to light, or the sound of her own breathing ticking in and out of lungs without much to say except "move."

In the car she had wanted to slide her left hand over his tweed pants and slip it between his legs, find a soft mound of flesh like unformed clay and mould it in her hands until it turned hard and sure. To whisper to him that there was no need to panic, his body would be beautiful on the side of a street corner hidden by a trio of maple trees with the seats pulled back. He entering her swiftly and she moaning with something close to delight but closer to forgetfulness, giving this man a body he has had to view for the last two months through his glasses. Watch herself in the rear-view mirror, her hands clenching, grabbing the end of plastic-covered seats, her hair pinned by the gravity of him, eyes reflecting it all from the visor and back again to her. She believed that would be art.

All these young men and women have art on their minds. She wonders if it's an art to keep still. She believes so yet knows they wouldn't see it that way. Only still-life. Two-dimensional is all she is with the illusion of three dimensions. The illusion of space and time held inside her flesh. In her spare time she flips through the science magazines her roommates leave around. The pictures are just as glorious as the ones hanging in art galleries. Planets caught in a moment of revolution. Gases turned into colours brilliant as a palette. She read once that eventually the world would squish together into one-dimension like putting together a cosmic sandwich, and then condense into a straight line. The energy of the universe would be spent up. Wasted. This kept her thinking for a long time.

Sitting is easier, though she dreads her legs and back drawn the same as the chair: wooden and static, symmetrical, sturdy, and firm. But when standing, the recycled air in the room gets to her. She has to breathe more deeply in order to stay still, and the third-storey studios have the poorest ventilation. She glances down at the first row and gets pieces of herself caught in her throat. A belly that hasn't yet been attached to ribs, pin-holes waiting to be extrapolated into eyes, a shoulder hovering as a planet onto itself; all these make their way up the page back to her. She breathes them in, wanting to give them another dimension.

Everything is white in the room. The walls, the ceiling, even the chairs and tables are white, as if the world were merely a sketchpad waiting for the artist's touch to bring her alive. Art may be the warping of dimensions, the way science is becoming an art. To stop the crush of the universe from happening.

The way she wants her lovers is like this. She likes the bottom, wants to feel smashed against the ground of whatever material they happen to be on, whether mattress, floor, or grass. She doesn't like it when they lift themselves up on their hands to watch her expression as they float in and out of her body. She likes the eyes to pass over, watch from underneath, farther down. And hard. To have that body grind over hers: the lid of a tight box. The feeling she craved was the same as when her roommates painted the apartment in the summer. It was so hot they wore swimsuits all day, letting the sweat soak through them. When the job was finished, with the leftover paint they attacked each other with the rollers. Squish from the sponges levelling her suit, legs, torso, breasts, stopping just short of her face. Wetness and warmth, yet the cruelty of the brush to flatten. Flatten into a white line. This was what sex was, what she wanted out of intimacy. To become invisible under the penetration, so that they were merely fucking a line. A single line of the universe. No longer even the shapes, the primitive shapes the students use as outlines for her: circles, ovals, triangles, rectangles, squares. She could be all of herself caught in a single line. Wasting of energy until spent up.

"Time's up," he quips, and the students evaluate what they've created, look back up at her for a final inventory before Drucilla grabs her robe, also white, to cover her like a blanket on a worn-out bed. Tying her belt, she then shakes her limbs a little to remind them to circulate. Her eyes, permitted to blink more frequently, spasm open and shut like a meteor shower.

He lists off dates for upcoming assignments. Drucilla rescues her changing-bag from underneath the table closest to the door and heads to the washroom. Today she isn't interested in sticking around after class to see the pictures. They are all the same. Basically she is given the same attention as the platform or chair. Pushing the door, she wonders if it was discipline that stopped the teacher that day. How it was he could stretch over the passenger seat with an open palm and reach to shut a door handle.

Later Drucilla will lay in her bed, covered in blankets, an open issue of *Scientific American* beside her. A picture of one of Saturn's moons, the crevices anticipating her penetration. They will seem as grey as the air. She will slide her five rectangular digits down to her triangle and her fingers will rub up gently against her the way a child uses scissors. Although it will be wet and warm, she will stay still except for that one hand, and she will feel cold and somehow dry.

At Your Service

In memory of Beryl Ann

Rodney managed to tie his laces and button his coat by himself and only needed to be told twice. He clung to Elsie, his cheeks flushed with confusion, not understanding where we were going, only that Mom was dead. And he rushed around the kitchen and living room, unable to sit still for a moment, repeating the news to everyone he met: Mom's dead. Mom's dead. With all the funeral preparations, none of us had the strength to scold him. What he said was true after all; Mom died in the night. Her heart stopped. She was blue.

The weather, for November, was unseasonably kind. Many of the leaves on your elms, drained of summer's oppressive green, were clinging admirably to their arms. The garden's withering stalks bent over as if waving or curtseying to an elegant arrival. We dressed the children in winter boots and mittens, but it wasn't really cold enough for them to catch a chill. The temperature had dropped ten full degrees. The mailman's coat was unbuttoned when he brought us a few of your bills and a notice from the dentist about an overdue cleaning. The blinds were half-closed to fend off the force of the sun. The frost sprinkled on the grass in the morning did not stay long.

Michael and I were in the city when they took you. We couldn't get out in time as we had to wait to catch a ride with friends, Michael afraid to handle the car on the highway by himself, and me without a valid licence. No need for one in the city, I know I kept telling you. Steven and your mom took care of you, or at least oversaw how you were handled. Your mom spoke to the police while Steven kept the children occupied in the other room with the television. That is all I have been told about the scene, except that it was Samantha who made the phone call and ran next door for help. And that she had been the one to find you in the early morning, thinking you had fallen asleep in the living room while working, the TV on mute. Samantha showed Steven where you had the emergency numbers posted, right by the phone. She kept pointing to them as if she couldn't comprehend how they could have let her down, how it was her mom was gone when she'd called the numbers like she was supposed to. Maybe she was even worried someone would blame her for having done something wrong. She found you, turned over on your side, your arms like folded wings, your face pushed into the sofa cushion. The children circled around us like lost animals, rubbing against our legs and jumping onto our backs, taking snacks from our hands. At one point Lenny scratched Steven, his hands tight around his neck like a corkscrew. The children told us about the policemen, how they wouldn't let anyone touch you, how they said they were taking you to hospital. Steven told us Samantha was crying *I want to take her, I do,* and the boys were scared. Corey wouldn't watch when they took you away. Rodney told one of the officers that you were wearing the wrong shoes to go outside. Your mom followed the ambulance to the highway. The children slept, oddly enough, like rocks, wrung out like stiff, dry rags. We stayed up all night in your kitchen, every night for that long week in those beige kitchen chairs, whispering.

Michael and I arrived in darkness that first night. Everyone else was already there, except Laura, who as you know had the farthest to come. Her plane was scheduled to arrive the next morning if all went according to plan. It did. As soon as I shuffled through the foyer, the house greeted me with the smell of tea as it did on every occasion when we were all together. I had mentioned once to your mom that the teapot was constantly steeping in your house and she seemed amused by the observation. It is something, I suppose, only an outsider would notice.

The teacups were filled, distributed quickly and efficiently clockwise at the table, in pattern with the past. Michael drank from one of your favourite mugs, the blue mug with the azaleas along the rim that you are holding in a photograph we have from a Christmas morning. When he is alone in the office, Michael takes out this photo and fingers it like a piece of old fabric from a treasured blanket. I know because he frequently forgets to put it back inside the envelopes that Laura sends us periodically when she has finished sorting through the doubles and triples she always orders at the photo-finishing shop. I walk in to borrow a stapler or write an appointment into his calendar and there you are, two-dimensional, matte, on the edge of the desk, your eyes fixed affectionately on me. Michael drank his tea slowly when we arrived, I remember, an oddity for him, as you know how he sometimes gulps too quickly and burns his tongue. I rubbed his thigh, my left hand underneath the table. He clutched my right. I stared at the clock you bought at the flea market along with a purple hat and a snow sled for the children. The arm moved jaggedly. It was alarmed. The house would stir until daybreak.

The children were tucked in bed. Michael and I had missed putting them to bed, and we were anxious to see their faces, to read them, though we couldn't even read our own. I kept turning to Michael as if I'd spot a code, a clear indication of where his grief was contained, and I would be able to mend it like a sock or replace it like a bulb, but my shock had not even budged yet. *The children*, we said, and it echoed across the kitchen from all of our lips like tender secrets. *The children*. Do you remember when you were getting ready for your first night out after the split and you told me how weird it felt to tell people you'd just met that you were separated? I said I hated the word because it made someone sound incomplete. "Well, I'm certainly not together," you replied, your head tilted back, chin punched out as you fumbled with the eyelash curler.

"You're the most together person I know," I told you. You were. You can rest assured of that. Michael told me often when an occasion was coming up, Christmas or Thanksgiving, or a birthday party or family dinner out, that not a single event could ever be pulled off without you. "She's the only one with a big enough house. The only sibling with children. And besides, she's the only one able to keep us all from fighting with each other." *The children* made way for *nephews* and *niece*, *grandchildren*, over the hours. What should we do about the nephews? What should we tell the grandchildren about funerals? Where will we all sleep, or pretend to, and who will lie down close to whom?

Knowing you, you probably would have laughed, thrown up your bony hands, and said sleep wherever you want and leave me out of it. Not once in over twenty years had your whole family slept under the same roof. That's what Michael said as he pulled his arms securely around me like a life jacket. You'd finally pulled it off. I could almost envision your childhood mornings. Everyone appeared accustomed to each other as they slumbered across the hardwood floors half-dressed, scrubbed of makeup and deodorant worn off, partly conscious eyes and hands scanning and feeling around cupboards and sugar tins to start breakfast. The usual adult decorum vanished. Your two

sisters and two brothers fell into a jovial pushing around. I scut-
tled between them. I spied your mom fixing Michael's pajama
collar. She even announced that it was time to brush our teeth.

Things to Do
Buy milk
Pay the gas bill
Ask Glen to look at the leak in the bathroom
faucet
Pick up Samantha after Girl Guides
Get video for the nephews
Fill out mortgage forms

Under the electric whirling fan, wrinkles vanished and tired
eyes were rubbed to childhood, weary from being up past their
bedtimes. The bathroom door opened and closed the years as
it accepted a constant hum of running water and unrolling of
toilet paper. Elsie called out for more soap. Steven said he'd try
to remember to put the seat down. Michael told me we were
delegated five minutes each for a shampoo. I asked your mom if
she could help me tie my skirt. It was as if time raced backwards
to catch up to you again, when you were all children and Mom
would sort you out like eggs in the morning, place you each in
your seats for breakfast, barely a moment to spare. I saw Death
do that.

Later on, after I'd rewritten the quick notes I took from the
night-meeting on what was agreed to for the various funeral
arrangements and handed them over to Elsie, I found Michael
outside in the backyard, your backyard, kneeling in his good
black pants by the brown stalks. I was shocked at first as it looked

like he was praying. But as I came closer, down the stiff grassy incline, I realized he was just sifting through the dirt in the garden with his hands. Then I worried about him ruining his pants when we'd only packed the single pair for all the formal events of the week. "She loved autumn," he said, when I reached the boundary of soil. "She loved planting with the kids. Naming the seeds and getting them all dirty and excited and ..." I remembered overhearing you once in early spring announcing to their eager flushed faces that they would soon see their flowers in the patch. Tulips, I think they were. Yes, tulips. You told them tulips didn't bloom for very long but that they were the prettiest flowers in the entire garden while they lasted. *Some flowers were meant to blush unseen*, it made me think of a line from a poem, a poem I could not conjure up for your service no matter how many times I leafed through books searching for it. Michael wiped his hands on the arms of his jacket, leaving brown smudges on each elbow, and returned inside.

I was put in charge of answering the doorbell, greeting the neighbours I had never previously met who came cradling dishes, directing them to the kitchen, thanking them for their offerings, answering questions about times and dates of services, then gently leading them out. We received food from breakfast until late in the evening, plates of finger sandwiches and vegetable platters, cartons of milk and juice, wine, fruit, entire cooked hams and deep-pan scalloped or mashed potatoes, cakes and tarts, cookies, pot roasts, assorted cheeses, and many dishes of cold pasta and mixed salads. The kitchen was littered with food, the fresh smells roaming underneath doors and through rooms, inviting, pandering our lips to eat even though we didn't feel like it. I tried to separate the foods that could be frozen and stored from those that would need to be eaten right away, and the fancy china from the plain Tupperware, the finger food that would be good for the guests and those that we could nibble at between the outings and errands. Conscientiously, most of the neighbours had attached a piece of masking tape to the bottom of the plates and casserole dishes with a name and address for safe return. Small communities, your Mom told me, know exactly what to do when it comes to funerals. They undoubtedly ensured that no one went hungry.

When Laura finally arrived, I was the first to see her. She left her grey suitcase and leather purse on the bottom stair at the foot of the porch. I went to retrieve them and she held the heavy oak front door open with her back long after I'd carried them inside. I don't think she wanted to cross the line. I did not take her hand and force her. Instead I went to sit in the living room where the boys were watching a cooking show and Samantha delicately fingered scales on the piano. When Laura then appeared, I was surprised to see how happy the children were to see her, as if nothing awful had happened, cheering and jumping around for the aunt who always brought gifts back from her trips to Europe or South America, who took them out for Chinese food and a movie to give you a needed break. Catching up on paperwork, bills, legal documents, and cleaning, instead of reading a light romance novel like you told Laura you did. How you laughed when you admitted your lies to me, and I promised to make you sit one day and I would pretend to be your lover, bring you tea while you soaked in the bath, lightly scented raspberry candles at your feet, and declare in my deepest voice, *My darling, your every wish, your every command is mine. I am at your service eternally.* You said you were looking forward to it, I remember. That you would buy a new robe and everything. You didn't believe me though. I remember.

For the visitations at the Westfield Funeral Home and Chapel, the same place they held your grandfather's and your father's, I arranged the pictures: your high school graduation photo, a bouquet of red roses and tassel tucked behind your ear; family portraits from department store studios, each child tilted toward you on wooden stools, green or blue fabric in the background; candid shots outside in the sun with the kids, hiding behind trees, poking out of rubber tires, paint on your jeans, in your hair; pictures on the church steps from Laura's wedding two years ago, your blue dress with the pleated sleeves; your own wedding pictures excluded. I tried to create symmetry in the design, something orderly and pretty, like fancy trim along restaurant awnings, to balance out the version of you, the turned-out toes and stiff arms like paper dolls linked across time. The same straight brown hair and small gap between your front teeth betrayed you with each smile whether crowned in a black robe or ripped T-shirt and pants. The only change, and the one that set you apart from the rest in envy: you got thinner with each child. I wanted to include some of the pictures you had drawn, taped up around the house like wallpaper along with the children's artwork, as snippets of you. The watercolour and pencil crayon figurines of women bending in gardens, seeking shelter under elms, leaning against yellow fences in the distance. You were at your best imitating landscapes, especially the array of oranges and reds in October and early November. Now that I think of it, you never painted spring or summer at all, did you? Only autumn and winter, and the winter scenes had an odd touch of snowlessness, streets of frost rather than ice, closer to December than January or February. Many of the photographs Elsie and Laura dredged up from the old cabinet in the basement I had never seen, never having known you married, never in your school years, never without your kids. And I thought five years of being your sister-in-law was a long time. It was just consistent. You were the mother, the sister, the one who pulled things together, the one with the house, separated, and paying the bills, running around playing hide-and-go-seek with glitter on your nose. I never witnessed any change. You got thinner with each child. As the photos grow more recent, you grow more and more to resemble the elms beside you, stripped of leaves, arms thin and bare. When the camera catches your green eyes, you are easily mistaken for camouflage.

Things to Do
Make this month's payment on the car
Pick up Rodney's asthma medicine
Buy whole wheat bread
Fill out permission forms for school field trip

"She was the only one to get those eyes," Michael pointed out as I pinned the photographs to the board with black magnets. "They come from Grandma." I was ashamed to admit that I had never noticed.

I want to let you know that I love your brother very much. I guess you know that, but I've never said so to you, or to anyone else in your family. It's never come up, I've never been asked. I guess it's assumed. I've always felt it strange how easily we speak the word *love* in conversation, but rarely share it when it truly matters. I love this hat. Don't you love getting mail? I love sad movies. But not: I love your brother. I love you. I never would have been embarrassed to tell you, I just never did. Michael misses you tremendously, pulls the covers off on his side of the bed and gets up in the middle of the night after not falling asleep, when he thinks I have, and I hear him pacing up and down the hallway that runs from the front door of our apartment to the bedroom at the far end. He wears slippers, but I can hear his heavy steps anyway. All of his grief is in his feet. I rub them sometimes while they are supported over the rim of the bathtub. His soles are hard, flaky. He says he can't feel anything when I pinch. I bring him a glass of whiskey with two cubes of ice. Steam collects on his forehead and I swear he is a blister, and I am almost scared to touch him in case he bursts. He plays old '70s rock music and hums with a voice you must have heard throughout his childhood, lacking tone, a nearly soundless exhale like a stifled scream. I rub his toes. I wash his soles. Sometimes, when his CD is finished, he asks me to sing for him, sombre hymns from when I was a choirgirl. But mostly he just soaks in the water and drinks. He likes it when I leave the door open a crack so one of our cats can peek in. He smiles then to see their timid, furry faces. I offer him chocolates and he pauses for a moment, but he never takes one. I cannot bear to tell him the porcelain isn't fooling anyone; he's sinking.

Since I was always too busy in the spring to get out of the city for your yearly reunions, I met everyone at once in a forced stream of intense traffic. Your first cousins Barry and Carl. Your uncle Brad and aunts Lucy and Belinda. Brad's ex-wife, Peggy. Donna, two other Michaels, a Linda, a Christopher, a Danny, a Mary, Elsie, Anna Lee, I think, or Anne Leigh, Judy, Janet, James, Paul, Gregory, Bob; others lost, unnamed, blurred in the shuffle. Arms moved, jaws spoke, legs walked. Mouths ate, lips sipped, bodies blended, people talked, we cried. I held on to those few names, I must have, because I know I wanted to and repeated several while greeting new batches of guests, while the appropriately stately but warm funeral host spoke to your mother to arrange any changes for the second visitation. Her name, I can't recall. I failed to remember so many names. "You'll have to meet everyone again some other time," Michael said. "A better time."

But I thought it was time I did, and I was placed at the start of the receiving line like a maître d' at the entrance to the salmon-coloured room, beside a small wreath of white lilies and yellow carnations, a pink bow at the neck that Samantha brushed against each time she went out to use the washroom. She had insisted on coming, though the boys stayed with your neighbours for the first viewing. She even once let me hold her hand and led me through the bright maze of flowers by your casket, reading the name cards out loud, wondering who some of the senders were. I couldn't answer; she recognized more of the names than I did. "Why do people send flowers when someone dies?" she asked me.

"To wish them a safe journey," I told her.

"But what if she doesn't want to go?" I just shook my head. I know nothing except flowers are pretty and maybe people send flowers so we can spot our loved ones in the distance as they are taken from us. Or maybe to comfort us if we can't.

I met some of your school friends and other parents, and the man you almost went out with. Michael spoke to him for a while, and I could see why you found him attractive, his tall slender figure, almost feminine, but with skin tanned like beige leather. Your mother held herself up by leaning against a high-backed chair, extending her arm out to everyone who came to pay their respects, moving her weight to whichever became the good side. Your grandmother — we were so worried she wouldn't be able to last — sat like a buoy, her large body and stout chin rising and falling with each breath, and the guests were pulled to her by gravity. When I brought her a glass of water to soothe her throat, she recalled my name. She recalled almost everyone's name on this occasion. Your cousins, aunts, even your friends. I saw Death do that. Make her lucid for this time. Make her sure her memory would serve her and it did then. But by the time we drove her home, it was as if memory itself vanished with you. She asked for her late husband to fetch her coat because the baby needed feeding. We told her she would be all right. Your mother said she couldn't wait to get out of her heels. Steven got their coats.

When we returned, it was my turn to walk around your garden, the wind dragging my shawl behind me. The night was warmer than you would have expected, too, like the week. The soil smelled fresh, and as a patch gave under my foot, I flinched. It felt as if I'd stepped on your grave. The loose warm dirt, the dry stalks, a yellow plastic ribbon that was meant to keep the plants separate, reminding me this was not my territory. I'd never felt right, you know, about the conversation we had here last year when you were turning the soil. Do you remember? That day I wanted to tell you about Orpheus, *my favourite myth*, I said, the one about the male poet and musician who loses his wife and descends into the underworld to retrieve her only to disobey the command of the gods not to look back and consequently he loses her forever. You were dirty, your hands and knees caked with dark earth, there had been mild rain the night before, and you were tired, and your cheek was scratched. "I'm not surprised. Men don't trust," you replied, pushing your palms deeper into the ground, uninterested. I let it go, secretly wishing I had brought it up another way because now I couldn't end it, couldn't tell you how Orpheus managed to survive, his body tortured and torn apart by a band of mad women, his head rolling down the river endlessly singing of love to the world. But thinking after the fact that the Demeter-Kore myth would have pleased you better, mother and daughter reuniting instead of husband and wife separating, and I promised myself that the next time we saw each other I'd try again. Another thing I never did, I remember. Why should I care about it now? You know when I was taken with Tennyson, the "Lady of Shalott" poet, the one I remember you liked, Michael protested against his poem "In Memoriam," agreeing with a critic who scolded that those who have genuine grief have little leisure time to write. Michael certainly doesn't, and all Elsie has time to do is scribble off lists before heading off to bed for a few hours' sleep. But I tell Michael to speak to you anyway. He knows I do. But he refuses, draws himself another bath. The only thing he asks is if you talk back. Sadly, I say no. He doesn't think you will.

"Heart attack?" we asked when the coroner's report came back. We were sure it was a heart attack. Inconclusive, read the report. Nothing foreign in your system. No signs of struggle. Nothing. The children were playing tag next door and we all sat in a circle around the kitchen table, drinking tea. Your mother phoned the family doctor. He said that these things happen. The body just decides to stop breathing. The heart decides not to beat. He was very sorry. Your mother gave us the news, the receiver dangling like a sick appendage from her hand. I had never heard of such a thing before, but we all felt better when he said you wouldn't have felt any pain in such a case. And through the white sheer curtain above the sink, when I turned to look outside because I couldn't stand to meet Michael's gaze any longer, to witness any more pain, a red elm leaf gave in to winter.

I should admit that not every moment that week was sad. I remember laughing a few times at the second visitation, but now I can't recall exactly why, except the mother of one of Michael's old friends kept telling me about her son's large feet. How she and her husband thought he was going to be so tall, but he turned out to be a short man with big feet. Her smile was contagious despite the occasion. Even Michael cracked up and slid his arm around my waist and squeezed. We stared down at our own feet, comparing them. This all happened while your children taped their last drawings to you on your casket. As your family worked out the details for the church service, I had distributed the paint and glitter, paper, beads, and pencil crayons, and supervised in the living room. I held Rodney's hand as he concentrated on making a perfect circle without using a compass. Let them spill glue on the hardwood table. Let Corey help his younger brothers with the scissors. Let them paste their stickers, use all the gold glitter, waste as much as they liked. Every once in a while I got up to wash my hands or pour a glass of juice or pop, leave them to their pictures and cards, and caught the hushed tones of "pallbearers," "limousines," "grandma will need help to stand."

"Love," Rodney asked. "How do you spell love?"

Things to Do
Make dentist appointment for Corey
Get birthday present for a nine year-old girl
Get Lenny new washable markers
Order the part for the washing machine

I gave him various spellings: *l-o-v-e*; *l-u-v*; a sticker of a bright pink heart. He chose the second and asked for blue beads. Corey and Lenny made paper chains of daffodils, yellow and bright with promise, gold glitter sprinkled along the bulbs. Samantha made her card conventionally, one paper leaf folded over the other, a message written inside. On the cover she drew a large house with a girl's face in the window, oddly reminiscent of your women leaning against fences in fields. I do not know if the face was meant to be hers or yours, but it was desperate to be seen.

The homemade cards framed your face while you lay in your ankle-length beige dress, so brand new that you had never worn it, waiting for an occasion or an evening out, your silver Irish pin on the collar. Your makeup was light as I know you would have liked it to be, soft white powder on the cheeks, forehead, and chin, and pink eye shadow, a matte peach hue on your lips. I'd never looked so closely at a dead person. I did not know before that your lips are sewn shut. I could see the tiny stitches, initially mistaken for chapped skin, once I permitted myself to focus intently on your face. Before yours I had only been to two other funerals, both closed casket. Curiosity overtook me. Approaching you after all but the immediate family had left, Michael attended your side with me, touched your hand, and sobbed. "Cold," he said. "She's so cold." I asked him if he thought you would mind if I touched your hand as well. With his permission I did, and I wasn't as struck by your temperature as I was by your texture. You were hard. I expected death to be cold, but I didn't expect the flesh to turn hard as clay so quickly. Hard and rough, lacking elasticity, and your hair, where our hands moved next, your hair felt brittle and crisp like ashen wood. "Her nails will continue to grow," Michael told me. "They'll grow even underground." I kneeled and made the sign of the cross and I think I asked you for forgiveness. Then I left you alone with Michael and perhaps you heard what he spoke.

As I held my winter coat in my arms near the exit of the Westfield Funeral Home and Chapel, I watched Lenny and Rodney try to keep awake, their heads bent against the glass window, flattening out their cheeks. Corey watched over them, kicking at their shoes and poking their ribs every couple of minutes to remind them we were supposed to be leaving soon. I wanted to carry them, but I didn't have the strength and they probably wouldn't have trusted me, anyway. Steven, arms moulded by tough labour, delivered them to Elsie's car. Your mother, composed and calm throughout the two evenings, after thanking the staff and taking a quick perusal of the guest book, deflated. We sat in the back seat of Laura's rental, the first and only time I have ever sat in the back with your mother. The age difference between us dissolved. Hands folded neatly in her lap, she resembled a skittish girl struggling to keep her manners. Corey rode in front and fumbled around with a couple of Rodney's plastic dinosaur figurines. Laura kept one hand on the wheel while the other stroked his hair. And regardless of my sense of our ages equalizing, I desperately desired your mom to stroke mine.

The other day I was working on one of my crossword puzzles. I misread the clue, filled it in because the letters fit. Saw after that it had read "Allayed Grief" and I had read "Allied." I inserted "Mourning." It was the wrong answer.

Things to Do
Replace fluorescent bulb in the bathroom
Chop wood for the winter
Get Lenny's eyes checked
Pick up Grandma's new walker
Apply for life insurance

When the minister rose and read from the Psalms, I felt Michael's hand shake. Whereas all of you only enter churches for weddings or funerals, I, with little knowledge of either, spent my childhood Sundays inside of one. It all came back. I was able to recite the words along with him.

The Lord is my shepherd
I shall not want.

Your pine casket, closed, surrounded with white and yellow lilies and tulips and forget-me-nots, lay, I could almost believe, comfortably amongst us. Your presence masked but unmistakable.

> Even though I walk through the valley
> Of the shadow of death,
> I fear no evil; for Thou art with me.

Michael's hand, his warm soft hand, between mine, the steady rhythm of his sad heart. I repeated the psalm in my head as the minister spoke a great deal I was not interested in about the afterlife. About accepting death and the blessed new life. I could tell Michael was partly impatient, too, but knew it was what mourners expect to hear. But then the minister added: "We must prepare for death the way we prepare for life." It was the only thing he said that made sense to me. Your brothers Michael and Steve, your cousins Barry and Carl, Paul and Laura's husband, Craig, who arrived just before the service, were your pallbearers. Your mom walked with Grandma, Elsie with Rodney and me, and Samantha with Corey and Lenny. You were buried in the plot beside your father. I assure you, in your final garden you were surrounded by love. As if we might be able to get through this. As if we might have been prepared.

From life to death the house you left behind is shaded beneath the words *as if.* As if the children still have a mother. As if everything can continue on normally. As if you are still here. The "as" conditional, the "if" hypothetical, placed on that axis of life and death like a girl balancing herself on a ridge of a roof slicked with rain. You were. We carry on as if we can. As if a mother can be replaced by the group of us. As if you had meant it to be this way in the event anything happened to you. As if they will not have holes in their memory. As if they should be calm and adaptable as animals, adults. Grow into you like hybrids. Trap those green eyes. And I lied. Lied because I didn't understand until now something else the minister said. Admitting you had never been a member of a church, he innocuously offered *bringing up children is a devotion*. I thought he was being kind. But he knew. As if one could recover from love.

Rest now if you can, if there is such a thing as rest for you anywhere. Rest, gold daffodil. Now you know what has happened while you have been underground. Autumn is almost ripe again. The green is the green left only for the aftertaste of memory. The children are asleep. When Samantha is older I will tell her about mothers and daughters, and how they trust they will meet again and do. I will explain to her the seasons. I will say Death does that. My sister, your seeds have been planted in the backyard and come spring, I will return for you again. I will.

Vertigo

Bottom right corner. Hit. *Bottom left corner.* Hit. *Top right corner.* Hit.

My accuracy is over 98 percent, even when the sessions run longer than one hour. I toss up the ball with my left hand, arch my back, bend my right elbow over my head, and serve. *Top right corner.* Hit. *Bottom right corner.* Hit.

The researchers love it. Even the poor, tired, neurotic, twitchy graduate students, whose clothes don't fit, and whose responsibility it is to supervise the monotonous exercise, call out target locations on the tennis grid, and check off each time my serve falls within the lines and within a 2-inch radius a "hit"; even they are visibly excited by my accuracy.

Good job, they say, and nod as I put down one of the research team's five tennis rackets—it doesn't seem to matter which I use, although I prefer bright yellow strings as they whip in front of my eyes, I still score the same—let them gather up all the neon green balls and head over to the shower stalls. *Good job*, like I've passed a test. When the truth is, I'm actually failing a test. And I have been for the last nine months.

I'm not a tennis player. I'm a diver. An Olympic-qualifying

diver with a difficulty range of 3 to 3.6. An Olympic-qualifying diver who won't be going to the Olympics. Because I have vertigo.

My father encouraged me to play sports and didn't seem remotely worried about my bat-swinging, ball-dribbling, bag-hitting, rope-climbing tomboy tendencies. In fact, he frequently took great pleasure in commenting on how fat and lazy the other kids on our street or at my school were. *People who sit still aren't really still at all. They're digging graves*, he'd say, and jump straight into the air tucking both knees, kicking out at the highest point (my mother lost weight without exercising. She could be found at all hours of the day in the kitchen, cooking up a storm, but ate like a bird. I figured she just grazed all day and never developed an appetite for a meal. Meals, for my mother, consisted of spoonfuls from each bowl and tiny cuts of meat; passing the salt and pepper and tubs of sauces; finding the longest yet most elegant way to move a utensil from the table to the plate and then up to her small, bow-like mouth.) then bouncing on his toes once he'd hit the ground.

A man close to 50, but tight and trim, like a coat rack. My father was a runner. Not a professional runner, but a daily runner. *There he goes, light as a feather*, my mother would say, shaking her head as she peeled carrots or sliced onions or marinated thick rib-eye steaks (I need my protein) for dinner, or organized my schoolbooks in the morning. *Always running, running, light as a feather.* And she'd shake her head again. *The best part of running is the turn home*, my father would sometimes say as he glided back inside for a quick reappearance if my mother had sounded more resentful than habitual, if, as my father liked to joke, her Latin roots got the better of her. Athletes appreciate habit and ritual, but not resentment. Resentment is for those who can't run or dive. And he'd kiss her olive cheek. And then he'd kiss mine. *Jump, Dad, jump!* I'd scream as a little girl. And he'd jump. And jump higher again. *You're jumping over your grave, Dad! You're jumping over your grave.* And we'd jump up and down, tucking our knees and kicking out at the highest point over and over until mother scolded us. *Don't you two dare talk so casually about death!*

But what was death to me then? What is it to me now?

I cared only for sports then. And what was that? A form of order, probably. Something aesthetic. Something you strive for, work for, push your body and mind to the limits for, something so beautiful you are almost destroyed by its presence, but you keep hoping will take you on, as it keeps shifting, changing, betraying, keeping you guessing.

After my shower, I'm expected to report to Dr. Leah Burhauer's office located on the third floor of the university athletic centre. She is going to weigh me, check my blood pressure, and then ask me a series of questions. Then I'm going to lie down on a blue mat raised on a platform to the level of her waist and she's going to manipulate my head in several directions. I will stare at her freckled nose while this transpires so she can monitor my eyes and see if they lose focus or twitch. During this procedure, she will ask me the same series of questions again.

Dr. Leah Burhauer does not like it when I weigh myself in the change room before stepping on the scale in her office — a storage space converted to office space beside the stationary bicycles room — such bad air circulation — you'd think grant money could fund something more modern and elaborate, but she says granting bodies don't care much for aesthetics, only for results. So I guess I'm a means to a result amidst rows of silver and black medical equipment on steel shelves. She does not like me weighing myself ahead of time in the change room because, no matter what, the two numbers are never the same. The difference is usually 2 or 3 ounces (or points of a kilogram — we note both), but sometimes as much as 2 pounds. On my 27th birthday last month, 4½ pounds. Calls were made, adjustments, a new scale was brought in and installed in the women's change room. Everything was properly calibrated, the procedure supervised by 4 university researchers and 2 equipment technicians. Dr. Burhauer looked as if her cheeks were going to crack — I've never seen such a stiff face on a non-athlete in my life. I wanted to say, *Anomalies usually please you. Inconsistencies. Against-all-logic results, no? That's when there are breakthroughs.* But I didn't. People don't like to have their words used against them when they're scared. And I could tell, for whatever reason, Dr. Leah Burhauer was scared, and she wasn't used to that emotion, though it rose to her cheeks and petrified there. Instead, I said things like, *Could I be losing weight — or gaining it — over two flights of stairs? Maybe water is drying out of my hair? Maybe it's my hormones — I'm due for my period. Maybe it's the vertigo? I could be unbalanced every time I step on the scale.* Dr. Burhauer could usually be placated with the last comment, but not for 4½ pounds on my birthday. *Vertigo can't be the answer to everything*, she said incredulously, though mostly to herself it seemed and not to me. *It just can't be.* And then, *This has no bearing on our research, so let's forget about it.* Her equally scared litter of graduate students, one of whom, the short Filipino girl who hiccups a lot, had just taken a cellphone photo of the scale reading as if it would not otherwise be believed at home, nodded to Dr. Burhauer and then to the others, but the nods had little conviction. Oh, I'm sure they all talk about me at home. I'm probably the subject of a great deal of dinner and transit conversation.

I wish those conversations were part of the reports. Not that I get to read them. I refused to get off the scale. 4½ pounds heavier. In less than 20 seconds. My birthday. With the same waist (25), hips (27), and chest (30) measurements. With the same shoulder-length wavy brown hair, and the same tight-as-a-cannon-ball calves. My shoulders, still broad from diving training, throbbed with strange excitement. My birthday. The day my mother gave me life. 4½ pounds. Where was it? In my long neck, my flat abs, my size 7 feet, my oak-brown eyes, the yellowish mole on my left rib cage? The nausea was swishing in me like a rowboat tied to a rock at high tide, but I refused to get off the scale. *Vertigo is not the answer*, said Dr. Bruhauer, and the graduate students, including the short Filipino with her cellphone photograph, wrote this down.

But I know vertigo is the answer to a lot of things. It may even be a question, too. But I'll leave that up to the professionals, the experts, the researchers. I'm no researcher. I'm just a damaged athlete taking work where I can get it. But I don't want to forget about it. Not like the way I want to forget about diving. I take a strange, secret pleasure when I slip off my shoes for a step on the stainless steel and watch the red numbers race to a plateau, waver, then rest in a stand-still position. The secret pleasure is in the knowledge that, in a few moments' time, before I can blink twice or serve an ace on the court, those numbers will change.

An athlete lives by numbers. And by belief in change. For better or worse, we're a series of calculations.

It was while running with my father through the ravines the autumn of my 12th year that I told him I wanted to concentrate solely on diving. He broke his stride, and his arms dropped to his side. He never did that — broke proper running form — not even when I would insist on taking out the basketball to dribble here and there on our run and he'd be forced to pause at street corners and on sidewalks to wait up for me, his knees marching high as he counted how many seconds it would take me to sprint to catch up as a wayward ball smacked off a curb or rolled down to a sewer and then back to his side.

Anything but diving, was his response, and took a sip from his hip water bottle, an item he carried, but only indulged in at specific landmarks on the route — the post office, the Hoppers' willow tree on Salter Street, the red plastic slide at the park. He drank heartily at those points, as if he were filling his belly like a pool. I loved watching his Adam's apple bob up and down his throat with satisfaction.

Water is life, I said proudly, as if to my biology teacher, flashing him my newly retainered teeth.

That's why it should be respected. Diving is a flashy sport. Arrogant in the face of nature. He resumed his running.

Without my basketball, and armed with youthful indignation, I caught up easily and began my offence. *So is running!* I held my head high as I kept to my father's steady rhythm on the long storefront pavement exactly 18 streets away from our own.

No, it isn't, he replied firmly, his white skin erased of its usual flush, handing me his water bottle, though I hadn't asked for it. *Running is an evolutionary advantage. Running prepares you for your finest human moment and to get you through the hardest human times. Diving will only get you into deeper waters.*

I was 12. Without knowing exactly why, I started to cry. Tiny hot tears streamed speedily down my cheeks. I don't know why, because my father was never moved by my mother's tears to go against any of his fervent beliefs (my mother would say, *That man is from a race of Vikings. They just go from place to place,* taking what they can. *They don't miss what's not there*). And I rarely, if ever, (*Nerves of steel*, she'd say of me. *She doesn't listen to pain*, was my father's point of view) cried. For me, tears were just plain ugly, like crooked teeth — and I didn't want those, either. And yet there I was, crying.

I have to dive! I'm really good. Coach Van der Berg says I can make provincials this year if I put in the extra training time! I was blubbering, talking and wiping my face along my sweat-shirt sleeve at the same time. My breath was laboured now. My father's long strides were pulling away from me. *You're the one who signed me up for diving!*

My father kept running. And though I chased after him, I could not keep up. But I heard him. *Your mother signed you up*, he said, without looking over his shoulder, as he hurdled over a speed bump and into the park, *to make a point. And now she's made it.*

For at least a year, as I trained 15 hours a week — at the university pool on 1-metre and 3-metre diving platforms on weekdays, and then at a training centre a 2-hour-10-minute train ride away on weekends, the nearest facility with a 10-metre platform — I tried to figure out what point my mother had won by my choosing diving over other sports. I begged her to tell me. She'd just shake her head and keep chopping potatoes or washing cabbage, and losing weight. With less flesh, her eyes looked bigger and bigger, taking me in whenever we faced each other. Her bow-like mouth remained mute on the subject. When I came in 3rd that year in provincials — to jovial cheers from both my parents — she exclaimed *You're so beautiful! You control gravity!* and I tried to decode her outburst for a clue to the puzzle, but I soon trained more hours per week, and more hours meant more competitions and less time for this sort of contemplation anyway. My mother didn't want to tell me. Fine. Neither did my father. Fine. Once something was decided, it was decided. I was a diver. That was that.

Did your vertigo subsist at any time during today's pole-vaulting session?

No, not that I was aware.

Was it better or worse at any point during the pole-vaulting session?

It was maybe worse at the beginning, but the difference between the start and the end is negligible, I think. I wouldn't know how to measure it.

What did you focus on?

Throwing my body weight.

Did you focus on the pole? Or on the bar?

Neither, as I said, I focused on throwing my body weight over the bar.

But where did you let your eyes rest?

I'm sorry, I don't know.

You don't know what you were looking at?

Not really. The vertigo makes everything so skewed and blurry. I just tell myself what I have to do and I do it. I suppose I see something, but …

Your scores today would qualify you for the Canadian nationals in pole-vaulting. Are you aware of that?

No.

It's time for another eye exam.

Okay. But I need a washroom first.

Are you experiencing vertigo?

Always.

Are you going to throw up?

Yes.

That's three times this week. Here's a washcloth. We'll weigh you again after the exam.

What I loved most about diving was the efficient beauty of it, the precision it necessitated from me. Calculation. Discipline. All muscles from my head to my torso down to my pointed toes working together toward the common goal of entering the water — first, with the most joyous acrobatics, and then with the most exquisite lines. My father was right. It was flashy, arrogant, to approach water this way. And throughout my years of training, I did pay the price, many times, the sting of my skin slapping against her face, my nose ballooning with her spray, my forehead whipped by her palm. There were times I thought the water hated me.

But oh, when she would relent, when you had achieved the feat of a perfectly straight entry, you felt her respect, you felt her welcoming you. You felt it by feeling nothing. The greatest moment in diving is when you've dived the water *parts* for you. You look wet, but you never feel wet. Not until the dive is fully executed and you've completed your last rotation under the water, in her arms, and are pushed up to the surface. You managed to manipulate all your weight into one common purpose and line. Weightless. Ideal displacement. That's why there's no splash. So exact, you weren't even there.

This week the varsity track, basketball, water polo, and ringette players will be participating in some of Dr. Bruhauer's experiments. I'm taking an extra 10 in the shower, water as hot as the taps will allow, trying to relax my muscles — particularly those on my feet — reminding myself to breathe deeply. Most of the varsity players have heard of me, either because I was supposed to be going to the Olympics in 53 days — hailed as a medal hopeful — a great pride of the university and the city — or because they read the Faculty of Physical Education newsletter where semi-regular updates appear on the vertigo-suffering national champion who has offered her body up as a guinea pig while she tries to find herself another sport.

After reading about these experiments, the long, gruelling athletic sessions, the tedious and sometimes painful scientific and medical exams and other corollaries, and the non-stop nausea, several of my former peers have stopped me: *Why are you putting yourself through this?*

As if training for the Olympics didn't push my body to unnatural extremes. *Maybe they'll learn something valuable. Maybe they won't. But I'll never dive again, so I need to find something else to do all day. And it pays. Pays better than diving.*

Then I usually laugh to put the questioner at ease.

What are they trying to prove?

They are trying to determine whether the vertigo can offer me any advantage — any evolutionary advantage, as my father would say — in any sport. I think the idea is that it's not only our strengths that can be cultivated to our advantage, but perhaps also our weaknesses. If only we pick the right arenas for them.

Do you believe that? many then ask.

I usually shrug, and say *I'm excelling at sports I've never tried and failing at others that were once easy for me. This interests them immensely.*

They usually nod, nervously, as if it's expected, though they have no idea what I've just said, but also a bit hopefully, the way people do when they simply want to believe in science and its results without any idea of why.

Usually, I nod back. Then I weigh myself.

• • • • •

I always knew my mother felt left out of the athletic life, but I believed it was her choice. Her domain was the house, father's the streets, mine somewhere in the middle — the natural world contained indoors. If she wanted to run, she could put on a pair of shoes. If she wanted to swim, she could buy herself a one-piece and take classes in any one of the city's many community centres. *Who has time for such things?* she would say to me, which would always make me laugh, since I felt like the busiest person alive, running to the pools, to school, to competitions, to the dinner table, back to the pools, to gyms, to my father's arms. But we had time, because of her. She never said this, but I know it's true. Time is its own kind of weight. I'm learning this too, along with the new sports.

I used to think she was a bit lazy. Cooking was easy. You mixed ingredients, but you didn't have to do the work yourself — the food transformed, you just helped it along, like a coach. I thought my coaches were lazy, too. Lazy because they had decided to stop competing.

Once, though, I caught my mother, her black hair tied back into its usual black ponytail, with two golden carrots in her hand, staring off into the window, the water pot boiling over on the stove. The smell was smoky, stinging. Her apron was sprinkled with dots of water, but she didn't budge. *Mom, aren't you cooking? What are you cooking?* I said, about to take the carrots from her arms.

Memories, she said. *Memories.*

At the time I thought she was trying to tell me she got caught up in her memories and so had forgotten about her cooking. This was easy to understand. I would frequently get caught up in my training and not hear a bell or buzzer. Once the fire alarm had gone off at the pool, and I kept swimming lengths until my coach hit me on the head with a paddle board. But now I know she meant she was cooking memories. My mother was too busy to run or to swim. She was in her own training.

My signature dive was the inward 3½ somersault in the pike position, 10-metre tower. When I say *was* sometimes, Dr. Bruhauer (and the doctors I saw before her who thought they could cure the vertigo with pills and convoluted eye exercises) says *is*, but I know even though they don't know (or didn't know) I will *never* dive again, even if in the end they do manage to cure my vertigo as they have managed to cure my broken arm, three ribs, and my whiplash. I loved the inward dives, probably because when I first started diving they were the most feared. I hated fear. I hated its smell. Diving smells like fear to non-divers, but not to us. To us, diving smells like life. Not death. At least, it *did*. I am no longer a diver. I must remember that.

Vertigo is not life-threatening, I am told by everyone who knows even a little about vertigo. *Neither are memories*, I want to shoot back, but don't. *They're not supposed to be.*

My mother left a note:

> *My memory has succeeded in destroying me. My body has continued to perform the same basic bodily functions that I've trained it to perform, day in day out, but my memory is stronger than habit.*
>
> *I feel ugly no matter how much I pretty*

*myself. I feel heavy no matter how much weight I
lose. I've tried arguing with death. I'm diving in.*

She shot herself. With an old silver pistol that belonged to
her father. I must admit, regardless of the news and movies, I
really didn't believe that people shot themselves anymore. And
certainly not women. Not women like my mother, who spent the
better part of their days washing, peeling, chopping, and mari-
nating in kitchens. I'd seen the gun once, in the basement, on a
shelf beside old woks and camping gear, locked in its dusty case,
and never thought about it. It was obvious my mother thought
about it a lot. She aimed it as her head, near her right ear — perhaps where the memories were, smashing them to bits.

I have been trying to tell Dr. Leah Bruhauer about the visions, but
she won't listen to me. And she has stopped weighing me personally. She must fill this part of her chart out though, I think, for the
grant money, so one of her twitchy graduate students does it for
her. I don't know why I think this exactly — I don't know how the
money flows or doesn't flow through this research centre — but I
believe that's the case. What I am sure about is that she no longer
wants to know about me. The result I am becoming is not one
she predicted, and not one she wants to continue working with.
She's like a coach who wants to drop a player. Not because I'm not
working hard, but because something has happened that makes
her no longer objective, no longer able to do her work as profes-
sionally as before — as if she's become emotionally involved. She
is emotionally involved — I can attest to that — she's afraid. The
charts (I'm now 50 pounds heavier than I was when we started
this, although my body-fat-to-muscle composition has barely

changed and I should be, by our measurements, about 10 pounds lighter than when we began) terrify her.

Last month, things went further. I told her that I'd been seeing things sometimes with my vertigo. Her eyebrows lifted. At first she was visibly excited.

What are you seeing? Spots of light? What colours? Dots? Flashes?

No. None of these.

What are you seeing then? Do shadows appear on your eyes? Do you have obstructed vision? (She took out a new notebook.)

No. I'm not seeing shadows or dots or spots of light. I'm seeing flashes of people, and objects, things that seem familiar, but that I know I've never seen before. The man I see sometimes, he looks a bit like my mother — his voice has similar inflections and he has her forehead and wide nose — and he reaches out to me a lot, his big olive arms, and I know I should like him, care for him, he's smiling at me, and he smells like sweet pepper, but I feel … scared … really scared. Then I see things like bags of potatoes and onions … I think I'm in the cellar, and I feel pain shoot through my whole body like an electric shock, but when I look at my arms or my legs or my belly, I can't see anything and it doesn't seem to be my body that's in pain. Is this some kind of side effect of perpetual vertigo?

So, you are experiencing hallucinations?

I guess. But I don't think they are coming from my brain, if that makes sense. I think they are coming from my body.

How long has this been going on?

Ever since I gained 4½ pounds on my birthday. Before then, I had vague flashes — a second at the most — but I figured it was just my brain processing the last 9 months, trying to get me to reorient myself (I've seen a blue pool for hours and hours a week for the last fifteen years) I thought it would go away and was not worth bothering you about. But now, now it's for 20, 30 seconds at a time. This morning, one of these sessions lasted nearly two minutes. I ran through a field, and could actually feel the nicks from rose bushes against my legs. I didn't care. I wanted those nicks. I enjoyed the blood trickling down my calves. I was crying, and when I looked down at my feet, I saw that I wasn't running at all, I had a stem in my hand and was beating my legs with it. What do you think?

I was seriously hoping that Dr. Bruhauer would have some insight to share with me. She's a doctor, after all. She does innovative research — at least that's what her website bio says — she must have experienced unexpected results before now. Before me. Perhaps she would start a new series of tests. Instead, she reduced the tests we were already doing. I heard rumours about her funding decreasing.

I suggest you use your medical coverage and pay a visit to Dr. Flin's office.

Dr. Flin? Don't you mean Dr. Phillips's, the neurosurgeon?

No, Dr. Flin. He's a psychiatrist. This is beyond the scope of my research. Your dealings with him should be kept confidential from mine. I don't want them to interfere with our tests.

That was 3 weeks ago. I had a session yesterday that lasted 47 minutes. I now recognize more of the people (they appear again and again) and the thoughts that take form in my head I'm sure are still not mine, but are very, very familiar. Sometimes I try to talk to the people in the visions, but it's hard for me, I'm not trained in this yet, and Dr. Flin doesn't want to encourage me. He keeps trying to prescribe drugs. Says I'm experiencing imbalance in all areas of my life — the vertigo is just one easy-to-spot physical symptom — which is making it difficult for me to cope. That I shouldn't be ashamed to be afraid.

I'm not ashamed to be afraid anymore. And I'm not ashamed

about what's happening to me. I'm less afraid today than I was those 3 weeks ago in Dr. Bruhauer's office. I'm gaining weight like crazy now. And I'm seeing things. I'm seeing things my mother left behind inside my body. That fateful day when I dove off the 10-metre tower. Inward 3½ somersaults in the pike position. That's what was listed. I felt the tip of my forehead graze the edge of the platform, and then I stopped rotating. I just stopped. I fell hard on my stomach. 10 metres. The audience gasped and the water screamed.

I didn't yet know what had happened. Pain. Shock. A stretcher. An ambulance. My mother's body would be found by my father following his early evening run, and after the police arrived at the house, the telephone would ring and my coach would tell him to drive to the hospital to be with his daughter, who had experienced a serious diving accident. I didn't yet know that my mother was dead. (What did that mean?)

But I knew I had displaced something. Or something had displaced me. It wasn't the water. I know now it was my mother. Her memories. Now, they are mine. They are making me dizzy, but I'll learn to deal with it, just as I've always learned to adjust calculations for dives depending on what platform I'm on, how many rotations are required, how long it will take to reach the water. Many people get dizzy when they look down on a diving platform. I'm dizzy when I'm not. But I didn't have these memories before. My mother's memories. I must figure out a way to use them. I believe she left them to me to continue her training.

She didn't learn to run until it was too late, my father claimed, weeping into his hands at the memorial.

No, Dad, I thought, *she can run faster than the two of us put together.* But instead I stood there, my neck still in a brace, and my left arm and ribs in a cast. I stood there, not crying, not because I didn't listen to the pain, but because I was more afraid than in pain. Afraid for him. And afraid for the deep waters my mother had launched herself into.

Take my father. He still runs, but now he runs farther, without a water bottle, almost to the point of absolute exhaustion and dehydration. *It's shameful now to me that I return home. I shouldn't. I shouldn't want to live so much.*

Do athletes have a greater urge to live than most people? I've often wondered about this. Are we living at our fullest by testing the body, by making our various parts work as purposefully and efficiently and yet, as beautifully, as possible?

My father runs corners like no professional I've ever seen. His legs are like grass blades in the wind — he's a natural, as if the wind is pushing him lovingly around the city. Nothing has changed that. Nothing.

The main thing missing now is a destination. But we can't blame the wind for that.

Dr. Leah Bruhauer is switching focus. I am to continue the experiments, in scaled-down versions, with Dr. Krissy Samson, a new tenure-stream professor, who doesn't yet have a large funding grant of her own.

At the moment, she is fascinated by my talents on the tennis court and in the pole-vaulting pitch, and she too is amazed by my weight — we spent an entire afternoon together stepping on the different scales all over the centre — hers consistent, mine going up, up, and up. I don't tell her about the visions, though. I can see she's not ready for that. She's far too light — like my father. Apparently, my mother's memories don't create advantages or disadvantages in the athletic arena. I'm not sure they create advantages or disadvantages in any arena, but there we are. There is much I don't understand. It's what I used to love about diving. Unlike running, there is no rational explanation for it. And yet, it's still beautiful, still something that seemed worth striving for. Though I'll never get back on the platform again.

I secretly hope they are never able to cure my vertigo. But I do hope they'll find a purpose for it. With every memory, I get dizzier, dizzier. And yet, I feel steadier, calmer, closer to the woman who loved me, who was no athlete, but who cooked and wanted me to make a point to my father by my diving. The woman who displaced her brains by putting a gun to her head, who thought I could control gravity. I feel her there, welcoming me. Like I once felt the water. I feel her without feeling her at all. She's so exact, she's not even here.

Acknowledgements

Many thanks to the editors and publishers of the following magazines and anthologies where earlier versions of these stories appeared: "Recipes for Dirty Laundry" in *TOK: Writing the New Toronto, Book 2*; "The Boy Next Door" in *Blood & Aphorisms*; "Wind Chimes" in *The Windsor Review*; "Sleepwalking" in *Exile*; "Three Days Left" in *The Fiddlehead*; "Blind Spot" in *Exile*; "Cover Before Striking" in *CVC Short Fiction Anthology Series: Book Three* (winner of the Vanderbilt/Exile Short Story Prize 2013); "Mycosis" in *Pagitica* and *In the Dark: Stories from the Supernatural*; "The Lilies" in *Humber Literary Review*; "The Man Who Loved Cats" in *Pottersfield Portfolio* and *Her Mother's Ashes 3: Stories by South Asian Women*; "The Still Body is the Perfect Body" in *Smoke*; "At Your Service" in *Existere*; and "Vertigo" in *Exile* and *The Exile Book of Canadian Sports Stories*.

A huge thank you to my agent, Hilary McMahon, for her unrelenting loyalty; and to everyone at Westwood Creative Artists. Thanks to everyone at Dundurn Press, especially Kirk Howard, Jim Hatch, and Shannon Whibbs.

Thanks to the Ontario Arts Council, the Toronto Arts Council, and York University for funding and other support over the years to complete this manuscript. Thanks to Graduate Assistants in English and Humanities.

Thanks to friends and supporters: Anne Bayin, Christian Bök, Charles Boyes, Diana Fitzgerald Bryden, Amila Buturovic, Barry Callaghan, Michael Callaghan, Tracy Carbert, Karen Connolly, Rishma Dunlop, Camilla Gibb, Linda Griffiths, Mary Ito, David Layton, Leigh Nash, Donna Bailey Nurse, Ann Peel, Dean Penny, Ann Shin, Dani Spinozza, Meaghan Strimas, Iris Turcott, Halli Villegas, Helen Walsh, Marg Webb. And thanks to Gloria Vanderbilt for the prize.

A special thank you to Richard Teleky, my first short-story teacher, who told me I had talent to burn. You've been a constant source of light and warmth ever since.

And lastly, to Christopher Doda, who lives with all my characters, and comforts us when the world does not always comprehend.